Freshwater Jar

Vinh Quyen Tang

Nghĩa Lan Nhân

Table of Contents

Preface

It's all my fault. Who urged me to keep retelling stories of the old days in Vietnam to my children when they were little, as I took them on walks through the streets, parks, or wilderness of Canada? But how could I help it? Every sight here seemed to remind me of something more vivid, more captivating, back there.

In a roadside puddle here in Canada, formed after the snow melts, where could you ever find a tiny fish wagging its tail and swimming about, like in a puddle back home after a flood? And in these ponds and lakes, where are the silvery needlefish, gleaming like a sewing needle trailing a piece of thread beneath the surface, or clusters of tadpoles, black as beans, playfully flicking their tails?

Now that my children have grown, they want me to write down all those stories I used to tell them. It seemed like an easy task at first, but the path into memory isn't one we can choose at will. Once the door to the past is cracked open, memories come rushing in like a torrent, carrying with them the long-buried aches and pains of a land that has endured seemingly endless wars and turmoil.

By borrowing these pages of 'Freshwater Jar', I hope to share a few memories, from my childhood and beyond, that have become a part of my life. More importantly, I want to express my deep gratitude for the magnificent blessings of Vietnam's natural world, which were so often overshadowed by the chaos of wartime narratives.

As a starting point, let us board the bus waiting in front of Firelogs Hamlet Market, just a quick 15-minute ride from the bustling Saigon Market, and begin our journey southward, toward the Saltwater Canal Hamlet. Let time carry us wherever it may!

Preface Footnotes

In this book, you'll find selected passages translated from the Vietnamese edition of 'Lu Nước Ngọt'. Where appropriate, additional context has been included to help non-Vietnamese-speaking readers understand and appreciate the material more fully.

The translation and supplemental writing in this book were completed by the author with significant assistance from ChatGPT.

Chapter 1: Catching Dragonflies

In the southern outskirts of Saigon, the sun glinted off the top of the flamboyant tree at the foot of the crowded Chà Và Bridge, casting golden rays over the Firelogs Hamlet Market and rousing the nearby bus depot. The market, named after the hamlet, had once thrived as a hub where mangrove wood from the coastal regions was ferried in and sold as firewood.

A dazzling patch of sunlight reflected off the bus window near where young Minh sat, waiting for his trip to begin. The steady calls of the driver's assistant loading luggage onto the roof blended with the cheerful chatter of vendors, filling the air with the vibrant energy of a new day. Moments later, the old bus creaked into motion, beginning its slow, 40-kilometer journey toward the Saltwater Canal commune tucked away by the Soài Rạp sea gate.

Before leaving the station, the bus paused at a street corner while the driver leaned forward, gripping the steering wheel and scanning both sides of the sidewalk for any stragglers. Finally, it pulled away, passing in front of the market and weaving around horse carts and bulky three-wheeled bicycles laden with baskets of vegetables, fruit, and chickens bound for sale. The bus honked loudly, carefully inching past the slower carts blocking its way. After a few minutes of careful maneuvering, it turned left and headed south, hastily crossing the Nhị Thiên Đường Bridge and leaving behind the city's frenetic pace. It then moved leisurely down the road flanked by vast, green rice fields stretching out on both sides.

The morning bus wasn't very crowded, and Minh quickly spotted a few empty seats nearby. A wave of anticipation swelled within him at the thought of reuniting with his childhood friend, Thành. The two had once lived next door to each other, but two years ago - when they were still in third grade - Thành's family had moved back to their ancestral home in the Saltwater Canal commune. Minh and Thành had grown up side by side in a Saigon suburb, their houses separated only by a fish pond that had quietly borne witness to the deep bond they had shared since early childhood.

Three years earlier, Thành's grandfather had passed away in Long Hựu Village, nestled in the Saltwater Canal commune along the Vàm Cỏ River. In his will, the family's ancestral home was left to Thành's father, Teacher Tám, who had been teaching in Saigon at the time. Teacher Tám promptly requested a transfer to a school closer to his birthplace, allowing the family to move back and live in the ancestral house. Only Thành's older brother, Công, remained behind in Saigon to finish high school and prepare for the Baccalauréat I exam.

Today, Công was going home for a visit, and Minh's mother had granted him permission to "tag along to play with Thành." Minh sat quietly next to Công, each lost in their own thoughts as the bus traveled south, crossing the Ông Thìn Bridge before bumping along a road riddled with potholes. The journey from Saigon to Long Hựu Island wasn't long, but for Công, who had made the trip many times in the past two years, the familiar scenery had grown monotonous. Seeking to pass the time, he turned to Minh and struck up a conversation.

"So, you two played together all day back then?"

Công was intentionally rekindling childhood memories between Minh and Thành. Minh grinned.

"Yes."

"I remember that, often after breakfast, Thành would disappear, and my Mom would say he'd gone over to your place."

"Yes."

Công leaned in, resting on Thành's shoulder.

"So tell me, what did you two do outside all day?"

"All sorts of things."

Công nudged him to go on.

"Alright, tell me one thing."

Minh didn't hesitate.

"Well, we often wandering near the marsh, scouting all the bushes to look for dragonflies perching on small branches to catch their preys."

"What's fun about that?"

Minh lowered his head, smiling sheepishly as he recounted how they used to chase each other, playfully sabotaging each other's attempts to catch dragonflies. Whenever one of them spotted the other carefully sneaking up to grab a dragonfly by the tail, they would quietly tiptoe behind their friend and suddenly shout so loudly that it sent the poor dragonfly flying away:

"Dragonfly, dragonfly with wings to fly,

Two little boys reaching to catch you high."

(*Chuồn chuồn có cánh mà bay / Có hai thằng nhỏ thò tay bắt mày.*)

That playful line was all it took to set off a round of gleeful chasing and tumbling on the grassy field. By the time they made it home, their clothes would be covered in dirt, and occasionally, they'd even get a scolding for it.

Poor dragonflies - long trusted as the farmers' weather forecasters:

"When dragonflies fly low, it'll rain;

When they soar high, sun will reign."

(*Chuồn chuồn bay thấp trời mưa / Bay cao trời nắng đập dừa em ăn.*)

But if one was unlucky enough to catch Minh and Thành's interest, it would have a rough time. The larger dragonflies flitting around the pond behind Minh's house were often trailed and bothered by the two. They would spare only the tiniest of dragonflies, as delicate as threads of colored silk with translucent wings that seemed to vanish in the sunlight, making them too elusive to catch. These little ones were constantly darting around and seldom stayed still long enough for the boys to pester.

Dragonflies come in a range of sizes, with the largest being the "buffalo dragonfly," distinguished by its robust body marked with green and black bands, reminiscent of an African zebra's stripes. Its head features two prominent, swiveling eyes, not only scanning for insect prey but also keeping a lookout for mischievous children like Minh and Thành. Most other dragonflies are about half this size yet are even more vividly colored. Some are a brilliant red, others a vibrant yellow, and still others a rich, deep blue. When perched on a branch or blade of grass, they extend their long, transparent wings, showing off their elegance. It's easy to see why the Japanese regard dragonflies as symbols of strength and happiness.

Children love catching dragonflies to satisfy their curiosity before setting them free. Yet, some - easily persuaded by playful older kids - fall for the trick that a dragonfly bite on the navel will help them learn to swim faster. Minh and Thành, however, didn't fall for this myth - not due to any special insight, but because their families, worried about the ponds surrounding their homes, had enrolled them in swimming lessons at an early age.

The pond behind Minh's house was expansive and connected to the Kinh Đôi Canal, a waterway dug by the French to link the Saigon River with Bến Lức - a key gateway to the Mekong Delta through the twin channels of the Tẻ Canal and Bến Nghé Creek. This connection allowed fresh water to flow in and out daily, nurturing lush vegetation along the banks and sustaining an abundance of fish and shrimp beneath the surface.

The pond was often covered with a carpet of green duckweed or clusters of vibrant water hyacinths, creating a haven for the plump white ducks from Mr. Tư's farm in the neighboring hamlet. When he herded them to the pond, their noisy quacking on the bank would suddenly cease as they plunged into the water, eagerly gobbling up the duckweed in sweeping motions, back and forth, until they had cleared the entire surface. During the season when the hyacinth leaves grew larger, Mr. Tư would paddle his sampan out to collect them as feed for his pigs. While out on the water, he would often scoop up a few small yellow frogs perched on the floating green leaves to use as bait for catching the large snakehead fish lurking beneath the surface.

While Minh was lost in his early childhood memories, the bus continued its stop-and-go journey, occasionally halting to pick up passengers. Approaching Cần Đước Market, about two-thirds of the way to their destination, Công turned to Minh once more and asked:

"What other fun games do you play? Tell me more," Công asked.

"We often go catching fighting fish," Minh replied.

"Where do you find them?"

"Usually along the banks of the pond behind my house."

Minh then eagerly shared with Công the secret fighting fish nests that he believed only he and Thành knew about.

Along the bank of the pond behind Minh's house, there was a row of coconut trees leaning over the water, casting a light shade with their scattered fronds, enough to shield the sparkling, natural ornamental fish. The fish glistened in hues of blue and purple, lurking near small openings woven by the clusters of roots that hung down like spread bundles of oversized chopsticks. Whenever the two spotted an ivory-colored cluster of bubbles floating on the water's surface beside the coconut roots, they knew the fish had made a nest. They would take turns standing guard, hoping to spot a beautiful fighting fish lurking nearby.

When they finally found one they liked, its fins gleaming as it lingered beneath the bubble nest, one of the friends would quietly creep closer, holding a basket in one hand and gripping the coconut trunk with the other, leaning out over the pond to scoop the whole nest into the basket. Sometimes they'd catch a fish, and sometimes they'd miss. Luck was simply part of the game. But nothing was more disappointing than the moment when, just as they thought they had a fish, it would suddenly flick its tail, dart out of the basket, and vanish beneath the soft, silky green algae with a tiny splash, leaving the two friends staring at each other, wide-eyed and full of regret.

As Minh finished telling Công about catching fighting fish, the bus slowly crawled to the last stop, coming to a halt in an open lot next to the ferry dock at the Saltwater Canal. Beside it stood a low-roofed thatched hut with two old wooden tables set out on the dirt floor in the front yard. A few men with sparse beards sat on stools, drinking tea and curiously watching each passenger step off the bus. Minh followed Công onto the ferry.

After the ferry trip, they decided to walk to Công's family's home, "to save on the cost of a horse cart ride," Công explained. As they strolled along, Minh glanced around curiously, furrowing his brow at how unfamiliar this countryside felt compared to his ancestral hometown in Long Xuyên, nestled within the lush, fertile soil of the Mekong Delta. He couldn't help but notice the absence of fig trees and white mangroves lining the dirt paths, as well as the passionfruit vines that so often offered a sweet roadside treat.

Minh recalled noticing clusters of water coconut palms lining the banks as they crossed the Salt Water Canal. What struck him, however, was the complete absence of the familiar water hyacinths that usually drifted lazily along the freshwater stretches of the Mekong. Here, the swift, swirling currents surged fiercely through the canal, a stark contrast to the gentle streams he was used to - currents so powerful that even a strong swimmer like himself found them intimidating.

The rice fields on either side of the dirt road were dry and cracked, with deep, wide fissures, a clear indication of acidic soil that, Minh thought, must make farming a real challenge. The only respite came from the steady breeze, which softened the otherwise unforgiving rays of the sun.

Despite the tranquil rural scenery, Minh suddenly felt a subtle unease gnawing at him. This feeling intensified when he noticed a buffalo in a nearby field staring intently at him. As Công astutely noted, "Buffaloes are used to seeing farmers in traditional black clothing," so perhaps Minh's white shirt was unsettling them.

From a distance, Công pointed out the direction of his family's house, marked by a tamarind tree on the right side of the road leading to the town market. As they drew closer, Thành and his younger brother Út came running down the road to greet Công, their faces lighting up with surprise and delight at seeing Minh again.

Chapter 2: Trôm Sap

Teacher Tám and his wife waited under the shade of the tamarind tree in front of their stately three-room house. The house, supported by jet-black wooden pillars, stood tall on a raised foundation that required climbing two cement steps to reach the front entrance. In the back room, a lavish, banquet-like lunch awaited Công and Minh.

Thành anxiously waited for the family reunion lunch to end so he could have some time alone with Minh and show him all the fascinating things he had discovered since moving to this remote part of the country. Once they left the kitchen table, Thành immediately led Minh to the back of the house. Within just a few steps, Minh found himself amazed at every turn. Although he often visited the countryside in the upper Mekong Delta for his grandfather's death anniversary, the vastly different scenery behind Thành's house left him astonished.

Stepping past a row of large earthenware jars neatly lined up along the house to catch rainwater, Minh was captivated by clusters of roots rising from the muddy fields, their spindly arms reaching into the air to support a dense canopy of dark green leaves.

"Are those mangroves?" Minh asked, his voice tinged with excitement.

Before Thành could respond, Minh moved closer to inspect a nearby tree. A sharp rustling noise startled him, and he instinctively stepped back.

Thành smiled and said, "Those are mudskippers."

Minh widened his eyes. Sure enough, there were two or three tube-shaped fish, jet-black and about the size of a child's forearm, each with a pair of eyes bulging on top of its head, lying motionless on the mudflat. Minh blinked, surprised to realize that some of these fish seemed to be on the higher parts of the exposed roots, seemingly in mid-air.

As Minh stared intently, he could hardly believe his eyes. He cautiously stepped closer, straining to see more clearly. Xuyt ... xuyt! There was no mistaking it: these fish seemed to be 'climbing' trees. They darted along the exposed roots, then dove into the mud only to 'run' further along the surface, trying to evade detection.

Excited, Minh turned to Thành and recounted what he saw.

Thành, unfazed, simply said,

"Yeah, they climb trees all the time."

It turned out that these fish could use their front fins almost like legs, allowing them to "run" on the muddy ground and even "climb" up the exposed roots. Minh's eyes widened with amazement - he couldn't get over this astonishing discovery.

Beyond the row of mangroves behind Thành's house was a low-lying area where saline water flowed in and out with the tides. As the water receded, Minh scanned the muddy field. Suddenly, he exclaimed, "There's a crab!" Thành chuckled and explained, "That's a horn-eyed ghost crab. People also call them wind crabs because they can move so fast, like the wind. They're different from the crabs we had near our old neighborhood."

A few crabs cautiously peeked out from the mouths of their burrows, their movements quick and fleeting as they darted from one hiding spot to another amidst the maze of holes dotting the muddy surface. Brimming with excitement, Minh recited a folk verse:

"The wind carries, the wind pushes; let's journey to the upland for wind-crabs,

To the river for fish, to the lowland for field crabs."

(*Gió đưa gió đẩy về rẫy ăn còng / Về sông ăn cá, về đồng ăn cua.*}

Seeing Minh's delight, Thành asked, "Interested in crab-catching, are we? We can do that tomorrow. Today, let's catch goby-fish instead."

Minh, intrigued, responded with a quick "yes" and followed Thành to the Saltwater Canal market. Passing by the tailor shop, the pharmacy, and the barbershop, they eventually arrived at the horse carriage station. Thành began wandering around the station, his gaze fixed on the ground. Curious, Minh asked,

"What are you looking for?"

"Horsehair," Thành replied.

"For what?"

After picking up a strand of horse tail hair, Thành explained, "We'll make a loop to catch fish." Minh quickly caught on and joined Thành in gathering a few more long, sturdy strands. Back at home, Thành used two bamboo branches as fishing rods, with the horsehair strands as fishing lines. At the end of each line, he carefully fashioned a noose-like loop. No hooks were needed; the two friends simply stood by the edge of the field, lowered the loops into the water, attempted to snare a passing fish, and then quickly pulled it up.

Fish swam abundantly, darting back and forth just above the muddy surface as the water rose. The little fish moved quickly, eagerly searching for food. However, this method of fishing relied heavily on luck. While one might successfully snare a fish and lift it from the water, it often managed to slip out of the noose and dart back in. Occasionally, with a stroke of luck, they managed to land a fish on the ground, only for it to squirm its way back into the water before they could lay hands on it.

Still, Thành felt that these fleeting successes were enough to rekindle fond memories of their adventurous experiences as neighbor kids on the outskirts of Saigon.

Minh had never witnessed a simpler method of fishing - no hooks, no bait, just pure ingenuity. Well, except for last summer, when he visited his family's countryside in An Giang and joined his uncle, Uncle Nine, in a fishing activity. It was convenient since it happened just at the doorstep of Uncle Nine's house. That morning, they stood on the front porch, gazing down at the shimmering water pooling in the front yard - a common sight in the region during flood season. In this area, poorer families built houses on stilts, while those more well-off built homes on high foundations, like Uncle Nine's house. Villagers needing to move around relied on boats, often moored right next to their homes.

Suddenly, Uncle Nine pointed down at the water pooling in the front yard and said,

"Look, Minh, there are fish swimming around."

It was the first time Minh had seen fish swimming right in the front yard of a house, with some even venturing close to his feet. Excited, Minh pointed them out to his uncle, exclaiming,

"Here's a catfish!"

"There's a carp!"

Amused by Minh's fascination, Uncle Nine asked, "Want to try fishing?"

Minh nodded eagerly. Uncle Nine disappeared briefly, returning with a slender bamboo fishing rod about a meter long and as thin as his thumb. Minh accepted it excitedly, running his fingers over each smooth, golden section of bamboo. "Must be brand new," he thought, admiring the pristine white fishing line attached. But one essential element was missing: bait. "For catfish, worms are the way to go," Minh thought, but he wasn't sure where to find any in the waterlogged surroundings.

As Minh pondered, he watched Uncle Nine place a chair on the divan, climb up, and deftly gather a piece of spider's web from the roof beam. Rolling it between his fingers, Uncle Nine approached and, to Minh's surprise, attached the web to a hook at the end of the fishing line as bait. With their unconventional setup complete, Minh positioned himself at the doorstep, lowered the line into the water-filled yard, and patiently waited for a bite.

By noon, as the waters receded, a delightful sight awaited them: two grilled catfish, expertly marinated in ginger fish sauce, were placed on the family dining table.

Minh's daydream trip to his ancestral homeland in the freshwater region, a hundred miles away from the Saltwater Canal Hamlet, did not escape Thành's notice. Seeing Minh's interest in loop fishing beginning to wane, Thành invited him out to the front yard to play "Đáo", a traditional children's game in which two or more players toss a handful of coins onto the ground and take turns throwing a stone to try and hit a selected coin. It had been their favorite game as kids. As they played beneath the tamarind tree, Minh couldn't help glancing at the slender, fingerlike pods hanging from its branches. Reading his friend's thoughts, Thành said, "Those tamarinds are sour; they're not good for eating." Minh asked, "Why didn't they plant sweet tamarinds?" Thành explained, "My grandfather planted this tree a long time ago. But according to my father, the water in this area is brackish, so only sour tamarind trees can grow here."

The 'đáo' game, a nostalgic reenactment of their childhood pastime, seemed less appealing now that they had both grown older. Minh looked around absentmindedly once more and suddenly asked,

"Do you remember the guava and plum trees in front of your old house?"

Thành's voice carried a tinge of nostalgia as he reminisced,

"Yeah, those guavas were something else, as big as oranges. Even the sour ones tasted sweet."

Minh chuckled, a hint of mystery in his voice, as he posed a question,

"Can you recall what else inhabited the guava tree in front of your house?"

"Just fruits," Thành replied.

Then, a sudden recollection crossed Thành's mind,

"Or perhaps you're referring to the paper bags my dad used to shield the ripe fruits from bats."

Minh nodded knowingly,

"Ah yes, now that you mention it, I remember those too. The gray paper bags hanging from the branches were a familiar sight. But what I meant were the ant nests."

Thành smiled, understanding his friend's intent,

"You're talking about the times when my brother Công used to poke those golden ant nests, aren't you?"

Growing up together since childhood, they shared a treasure trove of memories. Even now, such tales held them captivated. Golden ants often constructed their nests using leaves on the guava tree in front of Thành's house. Whenever Thành's brother, Công, fancied fishing, he'd prod the ant nest to gather ant eggs as bait.

Công's makeshift ant-poking tool consisted of a basket crafted from mosquito-net mesh suspended at the end of a tall bamboo pole. Standing beneath the tree, he'd nudge the nest with the pole until it dropped into the basket, then lower it down. Whenever Minh and Thành witnessed Công's exploits, they'd scamper away, fearing the wrath of the ants and the ensuing days of itching. Yet Công remained unruffled, holding the pole steady as the ants emerged from the nest, desperate for escape. Soon, they'd clamber onto the four strings suspending the basket, then onto the bamboo pole, advancing towards Công. But just as they neared his grasp, he'd tap the bamboo pole lightly, sending vibrations that caused them to tumble to the ground. In their panic, the ants scattered in all directions.

The two kids then dared to gather around Công, watching him carefully remove a few guava leaves from the ant nest to collect the ant eggs, which looked like grains of cooked white rice. They then tagged along with Công to go fishing. Công wasn't too keen on having them along because they kept playing around and scaring away the fish, as he often scolded them. But sometimes, since it was Công's responsibility to look after his younger brother, he reluctantly took Thành along. And if Thành was going, Minh had to come too.

Công brought along a round bamboo basket, about half the size of those that women carried to the market each morning, to hold the fish he caught.

Arriving at his favorite fishing spot, a smooth patch of land by the quiet pond's edge under the cool shade of a gooseberry tree, he sat down and baited the hook with ant eggs, using a tiny hook specially designed for catching gourami fish. Raising his eyebrows in concentration, he pinpointed where to cast his line, gently lowering the bait into the water, aiming for a well-known spot where he knew fish were plentiful. He sat still, his eyes fixed on the bobbing garlic stem used as a float.

When the garlic stem float dipped below the surface, he swiftly jerked the rod up, revealing a wriggling gourami fish on the end of the line each time without fail. Công carefully unhooked each fish and placed it in the bamboo basket, which he submerged in the water to keep the fish alive until he brought them home. That evening, as expected, a dinner of crispy fried fish with spicy fish sauce was deliciously prepared at Thành's house.

As Thành and Minh reminisced about the fun-filled fishing expeditions, Công appeared. With nothing pressing inside the house, he wandered out to stand by the front door, relishing the coolness beneath the tamarind tree. Observing the two friends playing their childhood game under its shade, he couldn't help but shake his head. "You two are already entering high school, yet you still act like small children."

In truth, the two, now on the cusp of adolescence, had begun to outgrow their old pastimes, including the once-addictive games of their younger years. Sensing the change, Thành invited Minh to explore the other side of his house and collect sap from the "Trôm" (Tropical Chestnut) tree.

Since arriving at Thành's rustic country home, Minh found himself continually captivated by the surrounding scenery. Each moment seemed to unveil a new marvel, from the exposed roots of trees reaching skyward to the scuttling wind-crabs traversing the muddy fields, and even the peculiar fish capable of climbing trees and darting through the swamp.

Now, as they ventured towards the Tropical Chestnut tree, a species previously unknown to Minh, his sense of wonder only deepened. This tree that Thành called 'Trôm' is as big as a small mango tree behind Minh's garden in Saigon. Its leaves are long, almost like mango leaves, but they spread out like the wings of a parachute at the end of each branch. At first glance, there's nothing particularly eye-catching about it, but when Thành led Minh to the base of the tree and showed him the pieces of resin-like gum embedded in the rough bark, along with the many scars, Minh found it strange. Thành pulled out a piece of milky-white resin, speckled with black dust from the tree bark, and handed it to Minh to see.

"That's Trôm sap, bled from the cuts on the tree trunk that you saw. It can be soaked in water to make a refreshing beverage," Thành explained, before taking Minh inside the house to show him several pieces of dried, hardened Trôm sap stored in a small box. Thành then poured for Minh a glass of Trôm sap refreshment from a large jar. Taking a sip of the thick, jelly-like drink, Minh felt a refreshing coolness, reminiscent of gelatin, coupled with the sweet taste of alum sugar. It was yet another delightful surprise for Minh.

Truly, it was a remarkable gift from nature. In coastal regions where the water tastes salty, rendering tamarind sour and other fruits like guava bitter, the availability of 'Trôm sap' offers a welcome respite. Providing cooling and refreshing drinks, it serves as a small but significant comfort for those enduring the relentless challenges of coastal living.

Chapter 3: The Ghost of War

After dinner, Minh joined Thành, Công, and their father on the front porch, where they gathered to enjoy the evening air. Út, Thành's younger brother, clung to Công's hand, laughing as Công tickled and teased him. Their father asked Công about his studies and life in Saigon, then turned to Minh, inquiring about Minh's family and old neighborhood acquaintances, who remained vivid in his memory.

Suddenly, the lively chatter and laughter stopped. A tense silence fell over the group as the adults exchanged anxious glances, and Thành's face froze in fear. All eyes shifted toward the road. A squad of soldiers, clad in black and camouflage, silently marched by in single file, long rifles slung over their shoulders, moving past the fence in front of Thành's home.

Mr. Tám lowered his head, sighed, and went inside, with Công quietly following, sensing that his father was thinking of his eldest brother. Mr. Tám's firstborn had joined the Northern armed forces in 1954, when the country began to split in half, resulting in two opposing sides, North and South, embroiled in a deadly civil war. Since then, no one had heard from him, and his fate remained unknown. In Mr. Tám's mind, however, his son might be among the Northern forces now infiltrating the South, possibly hunted by the Local Defense Force soldiers who paraded by his house each day.

Thành leaned over and whispered to Minh, sharing a grim piece of local news, "The other day, someone killed the village chief and displayed his head on the railing of the Cầu Ngang bridge. The day after, these soldiers suspected Mr. Tư from the upper hamlet, so they captured him, killed him, and displayed his head there too."

Minh felt a shiver run down his spine.

"That's horrifying."

Thành lowered his voice further.

"The vendors passing by even saw a soldier light a cigarette, stick it into the mouth of the severed head, and say, 'Have a smoke, Brother Tư.'"

As night fell, Minh followed Thành and climbed onto the wooden plank placed beside the family altar in the front room, preparing for sleep. He wasn't sure if it was the unfamiliar surroundings or Thành's unsettling story that kept him awake. Lying next to him, Công seemed equally restless and eventually turned to ask,

"Can't sleep?"

In the pitch-black darkness, Minh softly replied, "Yes."

Công continued,

"It's always been this way here. During peaceful times, people live with salty water and acidic soil."

He sighed and whispered, "In trouble times, it's even harder because we're so far from the center of everything."

Công was referring to their rural isolation. This stretch of land, at the ends of two historic rivers - the Cần Giuộc's and the Vàm Cỏ's - was a low-lying area near the sea where river water was always brackish, creating a challenging life for its residents. The soil was acidic, and the saline water made farming difficult. Even in alluvial regions with freshwater, farmers struggled, let alone here, where the land was resistant to crops.

Listening to Công, Minh asked,

"Then why did Uncle Tám move back here?"

"After my grandfather passed away, my father was the only son left. My two uncles had already died in the resistance against the French. My father said, 'If we don't return, who will tend to our ancestors' graves?'"

Minh thought, "So, to protect his ancestors' resting place, Mr. Tám willingly left the comfort of the freshwater region to endure the salty, acidic soil of his homeland." As he reflected further on the resilience of those who had made their lives on this unforgiving land, Minh felt a deep admiration for these people - who, for generations, had clung to the soil, standing at the frontlines of hardship, faithfully upholding their ancestors' wisdom:

"*Never abandon the fields,*

Every inch of land is worth its weight in gold."

(*Ai ơi đừng bỏ ruộng hoang / Bao nhiêu tấc đất, tấc vàng bấy nhiêu.*)

Minh suddenly remarked, "Thanks to those who came before us - enduring all the hardships of this land - we have the country we do today, don't we?"

Công chuckled with admiration.

"You're still young, but you already think that way."

In the stillness of the night, on land still warm with the steps of his ancestors, Minh felt the weight of his grandmother's words - words she repeated after every meal: never to leave a single grain of rice in the bowl, so as not to "sin against the farmers who toiled in the fields." As sleep slowly overtook him, he pictured her familiar figure: silver-haired, seated at the kitchen table, pausing before and after each meal to lift her chopsticks in prayer, three times, offering solemn gratitude for the labor of those who worked the land.

Chapter 4: Chasing Wind Crabs

Before dawn, the sounds of vendors hauling chickens, ducks, vegetables, and other goods to the market woke Minh. Công stepped out into the yard to exercise, while Minh lay still, waiting for Thành to wake up and start a new day. As soon as he saw Thành stir, Minh nudged him, urging,

"Get up quickly, let's go pick rose apples (trái lý)!"

Thành groaned, "There aren't any rose apples to pick here."

The secret adventures of children are often unknown to adults. When Thành and Minh were young and living in Saigon, their house was across from a temple. In front of the temple, on the wall of the main hall, there was a painting of Buddha Shakyamuni, robed in gold and entering Nirvana. Locals called this temple the Reclining Buddha Temple to distinguish it from another temple on the same street, known as the Standing Buddha Temple, which featured a statue of Avalokitesvara.

In the courtyard of the Reclining Buddha Temple was a Buddhist school, housed in a building painted with yellow lime. Right behind the temple gate stood an old rose apple tree with lush branches that nearly obscured the school's nameplate. Passersby could catch the faint fragrance of its fruits even before seeing the tree. The rose apples were about the size of a plum (trái mận) but round, like the alms bowls that monks carried. The taste was similar to that of a plum but much sweeter, and it had a distinct fragrance that lingered in the nose.

The enticing flavor of the rose apples was enough to wake Thành and Minh early on mornings after heavy rains and strong winds, prompting them to run to the temple gate and gather fallen fruits from the grassy courtyard. Often, however, Mr. Tạ, the temple caretaker, had already collected them and set them aside in a paper bag for the two kids. Sometimes, though, he would open the temple gate and let them pick the large, ripe fruits directly from the tree to take home and enjoy.

Now, although there were no such sweet fruits to pick in the Saltwater Canal region, Thành tried to please his friend by waking up early, asking his mother for money, and taking Minh to the market for breakfast snacks. Minh, thinking he was just going out with his friend, didn't expect any specialties like Mỹ Tho noodle soup or Cai Lậy rice porridge, which he usually had during family trips to his homeland along the Mekong River. To his surprise, the Saltwater Canal market also had many delicious treats waiting to be discovered, especially the banana leaf-wrapped 'bánh tằm'. These chewy cassava noodles, colored green by pandan leaf extract and red by beetroot, were topped with finely grated coconut and dotted with inviting black sesame seeds. One bite of this treat sent the fragrance of sesame to the nose and the rich flavor of coconut milk to the tongue, leaving Minh craving more.

After they ate, Thành suggested taking Minh to his aunt's house.

"There's nothing much around here, but my aunt has a crab apple tree."

Minh's curiosity was piqued.

"What's a crab apple? I've never seen one before."

"The tree at my aunt's house is as big as the guava tree that used to be in front of my house, but it's loaded with fruit."

"Is the fruit anything like a French apple?"

"Kind of. It has a similar shape but is much smaller - only about the size of your thumb."

When they arrived, Minh stood in fascination, staring at the tiny crab apples hanging in thick clusters from the branches. They looked enticing, but the moment Minh picked one and took a bite, he understood why the tree was still heavy with fruit. The taste was bitter, and even the birds left them alone. It couldn't compare to guavas, not even the young ones from the tree in front of Thành's old house, which they sometimes picked to snack on when they were bored. Nor did it have the satisfying tang of the cork tree fruits along the riverbank, which, at least, could be dipped in chili salt to satisfy a craving.

Minh didn't have to feel disappointed for long because Thành was already eager to lead him down another memory lane. Soon, they returned home, each grabbing a tin can before heading to Uncle Tư's field - a relative of Thành's - to catch crabs. They walked along the narrow dirt road by the canal, bordered by a line of nipa palm trees under the soft morning sunlight. Memories unexpectedly flooded back, and Minh asked Thành,

"Do you remember how we used to wander around the pond banks looking for needlefish?"

Minh was referring to the thin, glistening fish in the water that looked like silver needles, with short threads trailing behind as they flicked their tails.

Thành nodded with a smile.

"Yeah, we tried so hard to catch them and keep them in jars to play with at home, but we rarely succeeded."

Minh suddenly remembered,

"Tadpoles were the easiest to catch, but do you remember that one time your dad scolded us for it?"

Thành laughed, recalling,

"After that, I even caught some toad eggs and put them in my dad's drinking glass. I got scolded again."

Minh chuckled.

"Why don't I remember that?"

Thành explained,

"I think you'd already gone back to your hometown by then. I stayed behind, wandering around the ponds we used to visit. I saw a string of toad eggs by the pond near your house, scooped them up, and put them in my dad's glass just to look at them."

The clusters of toad eggs, resembling soaked vermicelli, looked translucent except for speckled black dots. Each dot would hatch into a tadpole, a tiny black bean with a vigorously wagging tail. What child wouldn't be fascinated by that? After a few days, as their tails fell off, they would transform into tiny toads and hop onto the shore.

As the two walked past the row of nipa palms, a distressing sight unfolded before them: severe riverbank erosion had left two old tamanu trees with half of their roots exposed to the air, clutching onto what little soil remained. A tangled mass of large and small roots hung dried in the air, a pitiful scene. Minh sighed,

"The land has eroded a lot."

Thành looked at the rushing water.

"My dad says it's because the French dug this canal too wide back in the day, so the strong water flow keeps washing the soil away."

"That makes sense. The other day, when I was crossing the ferry, I noticed how fast the water was flowing. There were big waves too. It's really dangerous. Why did they dig such a big canal?"

"I heard they had to dig the canal so deep and wide for their warships to pass through."

"That's strange. French ships used to sail through here?" Minh asked, surprised.

"Since we were born and raised in Saigon, we wouldn't know," Thành replied. "But ever since I came here, I've heard my dad and other elders talking about fighting the French along these river stretches."

Thành gazed into the distance, raising his eyebrows as he tried to recall the stories he'd heard.

"In fact, back then, we did hear about the hero Nguyễn Trung Trực burning the French ship 'Espérance' at the river mouth 'Nhựt Tảo'. But it always sounded like a distant fairy tale. Being here, I feel much closer to history."

As he spoke, Thành pointed ahead.

"From this section of the Vàm Cỏ River, we can go upstream on the Vàm Cỏ Đông River to reach the river mouth of Nhựt Tảo, where that historic battle took place."

Thành was referring to one of the two celebrated battles against the French led by the hero Nguyễn Trung Trực, often memorialized in folklore through two immortal verses:

"Fire at Nhựt Tảo shakes heaven and earth;

Sword unsheathed at Kiên Giang frightens ghosts and gods."

(*Hỏa hồng Nhựt Tảo kinh thiên địa / Kiếm bạt Kiên Giang khấp quỷ thần.*)

The second battle was when he and his militia ambushed the French garrison at Kiên Giang.

Minh understood Thành's point. Standing at the frontier, it was hard not to feel the sacred spirit of the land. Thành continued,

"If only you could stay here longer, I'd take you to see the Rạch Cát Fort left by the French."

"Is it like the French fort in Bình An, close to our place in Saigon?"

"No, the Rạch Cát Fort here is much larger."

In the early 20th century, after decades of conflict between the French and the Nguyễn dynasty's forces - starting with the capture of Gia Định Citadel and ongoing battles with anti-French uprisings in what the French called Cochinchina - the French fortified key locations to protect their stronghold in the region. Among these was the Bình An fort, mentioned by Minh, which lay near his and Thành's childhood home. This fort, constructed on the left bank of the Kinh Đôi canal near the Bà Lớn waterway, was a robust concrete structure designed to defend Saigon's southwestern perimeter. Its primary purpose was to prevent resistance forces from infiltrating the city from the western provinces, although its narrow location limited its firepower to smaller groups.

Another significant fort was the Rạch Cát Fort in Long Hựu Đông, which Thành wished he could show his friend. Positioned strategically near the Soài Rạp estuary, where the Cần Giuộc and Vàm Cỏ rivers merge with the Soài Rạp River, this fort was a large and heavily fortified checkpoint. Equipped with powerful artillery with a range of several kilometers, its purpose was to thwart anti-French forces coming from the Mekong Delta, following traditional routes. These routes once served the Nguyễn dynasty in efforts to reclaim Gia Định Citadel during earlier civil conflicts. From bases like the Mỹ Tho fort and Long Hồ palace in Vĩnh Long, royal forces had once navigated the intricate river systems of the Mekong Delta, advancing through the Vàm Cỏ and Soài Rạp Rivers toward the citadel, located near what later became Saigon.

Thành continued,

"The French fort near our house back then was like a small bunker, just four sturdy walls with a few embrasures. But the Rạch Cát Fort here is different - it has two massive fortresses, equipped with cannons, various artillery, and machine guns."

Minh clicked his tongue, "It's a shame we can't go see it."

Thành went on, "My dad said the cannons at Rạch Cát could reach Gò Công to the west and Cần Giờ to the east. If needed, the heavy artillery could even fire as far as the mouth of the Lòng Tảo River or further to support the three coastal defense forts in Vũng Tàu, preventing other European colonial powers from encroaching on French-held Vietnam."

Following Thành's direction, Minh gazed into the distance. Amid the vast fields and rivers, he tried to picture the grand landscape of their homeland. He was surprised to find himself, even at the age of ten, experiencing a moment of poetic reflection akin to the sentiment of the poet Tản Đà: '*I stand here, gazing at our country map.*' (*Nọ bức dư đồ thử đứng coi.*)

Minh walked in thoughtful silence, reflecting on those who had come to this remote, challenging land to reclaim it and establish settlements, as well as the generations who had sacrificed to protect their homeland. The more formidable the enemy's fortresses and the fiercer the invaders' weaponry, the more they underscored the valiant resistance of his ancestors. Each French fortress scattered across the country stood as a reminder of the boundless sacrifices made by countless generations, who poured their hearts and souls into defending their land against the invaders' iron and steel, protecting every inch of their homeland.

Minh had never imagined that this seemingly isolated place, which 'brother' Công had once called "far from the sun," could hold such a profound connection to the history of his nation's founding and defense.

The wind from the East Sea blew fiercely as the two brothers walked along the canal bank, feeling as if they were teetering on the edge of a cliff. The riverbank wasn't lush with the soft greenery that usually embraced the peaceful waters near Minh's maternal grandparents' home. Instead, it was red like baked bricks, exposing raw earth as if stripped bare. In the vast silence, a large house loomed in the distance. As they drew closer, an unusually bustling scene for this remote area gradually came into view. In front of the house, four men worked busily among scattered planks and wooden boards, while a group of children played nearby. Minh thought it must be a sawmill, given the sounds of sawing and hammering.

Noticing the question in Minh's curious eyes, Thành explained, "It's a coffin-making place."

"They're making coffins?" Minh asked.

"Yes. This place is near my Uncle Tư's house. He passes by here every day and often says the coffin-making business seems to be doing well around here."

Minh was taken aback by the remark's irony. Perhaps it was because he had never thought of coffin-making as just another trade, or maybe because his young mind couldn't reconcile the image of death with the implied satisfaction of profit in Uncle

Tư's comment. Yet, after the initial shock, Minh realized that Uncle Tư's words hinted at a harsh reality in this poor region.

Though Minh had only been in Thành's hometown for two days, he noticed that, aside from the bustling market, the coffin workshop was the only other place alive with activity. As they walked past its yard, Minh observed curiously. A middle-aged man, with a scarf tied around his head, had one foot propped on a wooden stand, holding a plank in one hand while vigorously sawing with the other. Nearby, an older man was carefully applying red paint to a coffin lid. A younger man, likely the third generation in the family, was filling the gaps between the wooden planks of a coffin. Four children were playing tag, chasing a flock of chickens around the yard.

Minh wondered aloud, "Why do they make so many coffins here when the population is quite sparse?"

Thành put a finger to his lips, signaling Minh to lower his voice, then leaned closer and whispered, "People die every day. One day, men from the other side come and kill someone here. The next day, soldiers come looking and kill someone from the other side."

"That's horrible," Minh murmured, shaking his head in sadness.

The two friends reached the entrance of the coffin workshop. Thành shot a sideways glance at Minh, a smirk creeping across his face. "Why are you walking so fast? Are you scared?"

Minh shook his head, trying to sound confident. "No, I'm not scared."

But Thành's teasing stirred up memories in Minh's mind. He chuckled, nudging his friend. "Remember how we used to dare each other to ride down the Ngang Bridge?"

The Ngang Bridge sat in front of the police station near where they grew up. Back then, they were only seven. Minh's father had bought him a small bicycle, just knee-high to an adult. Though it was Minh's bike, they both rode it - one steering and pedaling, the other holding tight around the rider's waist. At first, they stayed close, riding up and down the paved road in front of their houses, nearly two hundred meters long and bracketed by canals on either end. Even at the farthest edge, they could still glimpse the hibiscus hedge in front of Thành's house, a reassuring sight. They favored the stretch taking them to the Kinh Đôi canal, where the road was quieter, and fewer people passed by.

After a few days, each time they reached the end of the road, Thành nudged Minh to keep going along the canal path, urging him to venture further. At first, Minh refused, gripped by his fear of the forbidden area ahead - Bãi Sậy Police Station. Although the French colonial regime in Vietnam had ended and French troops had withdrawn a year prior, the place still felt haunted, and "restless spirits" were said to linger there, at least according to the whispered stories of the adults, which echoed in the children's minds. They'd heard of the moans of prisoners drifting from the jail each night, the cries for help from Uncle Ba, tied under the bridge to drown with the rising tide, the last pleas of Uncle Hai, executed beside the bridge pier, and the laments of Auntie Tư, who was brutalized and discarded among the mangroves by the riverbank. The nightmare of the colonial era had not yet released its hold.

Each day after that, as they reached the intersection, Thành would prod Minh to keep going. Whether worn down by Thành's persistence or tired of the initial route's familiarity, Minh finally agreed, though he set a new limit: they would only ride to the water fountain, about 20 meters past the intersection. But it didn't take long before Thành, emboldened as ever, pushed to extend their path, doubling the distance from the fountain to reach Mr. Sáu's café before turning back. Both knew this was the final boundary; beyond lay the bunker at the southeast corner of the dreaded police station. But for Thành, known as the "bravest of the family," no boundary - real or imagined - seemed capable of restraining him.

It didn't take long for Thành to hatch a daring plan: they would bike past the Bãi Sậy police station, climb to the top of Ngang Bridge, then turn around and race downhill, letting the bike coast freely without pedaling. No child could resist the thrill of such a ride, so it was no surprise when "riding downhill" quickly became the highlight of their summer. Sitting motionless on the bike, eyes wide with excitement, they savored the rush of the moment, feeling as if they were soaring beyond the universe and all earthly bounds. Together, they transformed old fears into joyful, lasting memories that would mark the early years of their friendship.

Minh was lost in thought when Thành pointed ahead and said, "There's my uncle Tư's house."

Not long after passing the coffin workshop, they arrived at the front of Uncle Tư's home. The spacious, tiled-roof house stretched across three sections, similar to other well-off families, though it wasn't as grand as Thành's. The front columns were relatively slender, and there were no doors visible, allowing the sea breeze to flow freely from the back to the front. Uncle Tư, dressed in a white *bà ba* (a traditional shirt) that matched his silvery hair and beard, sat on a wooden platform by the side of the house, meticulously mending a fishing net. In the family, he was affectionately known as Mr. Tư "Tiên," or "Fairy Tư," a nickname bestowed by Thành. When Thành was a child, he would exclaim, "Uncle Tư looks like a fairy!" captivated by his uncle's white hair and beard.

Thành greeted Uncle Tư and introduced Minh before stepping closer to his uncle. "Are you mending the net for fishing?" he asked.

"I haven't been fishing for two years now - too old for it," Uncle Tư replied, glancing up at Thành. "I'm fixing this net to give to Hai's son, you know, 'The Boatman,' as folks call him," he added.

Hai, though technically a resident of the upper village, spent more time on his boat than on land. His family owned a cargo boat that transported food and goods to various markets in the region, from Cần Giuộc Market to Saltwater Canal Market and beyond. A few days ago, Uncle Tư had the chance to hitch a ride on Hai's boat to Long An. In the evening, everyone gathered on the front deck, where Hai's family treated Uncle Tư to an unforgettable meal of 'cá linh' fish porridge.

Uncle Tư recalled, "Hai's wife had a pot of rice porridge ready. As soon as it was cooked, their child cast a net into the river and pulled up some fresh 'cá linh' fish. Hai scooped up a basin of the fish and dropped each one straight into the boiling porridge…"

Minh interrupted in surprise, "They hadn't prepared the fish at all?"

Uncle Tư answered with a mouth-watering smile, still savoring the memory of that special treat. "No need to do anything to the fish. Hai just stands by the pot, skimming off any foam as it forms, throwing it away. Yet the porridge is incredibly tasty. Take it with a sip of rice wine, and you feel like you're in heaven."

Uncle Tư lifted his gaze, letting his mind drift along with the freshwater of the Cần Giuộc River, a refreshing current for his memories. After a moment, when the taste of the porridge had faded in his mind, he noticed the two children standing nearby with cans in their hands.

"You two," he urged, "go to the backyard and catch some wind crabs."

Thành and Minh quickly thanked Uncle Tư and followed the path beside the house to the backyard. Just past the rainwater jar at the corner, Minh's eyes widened as he began pointing frantically in all directions, shouting to Thành, "There's a crab! There's another crab!"

On the muddy bank near the water coconut (Nipa palm) trees, a few tiny wind crabs scuttled back and forth, each brandishing an oversized claw as they moved along. It truly is a paradise of childhood, at least for Thành and Minh. Although there aren't any vegetable beds or chili plants like those by Uncle Hai's house next door - where they'd wander as they grew up, hunting for little round green beetles or their long-bodied cousins with shiny, yellow-tinted wings glistening under the ever-bright sun - this place still holds its magic. There are no mint patches, lush purslane, or the vibrant pennywort covering Uncle Bảy's garden, nestled behind rows of pearl plants dotted with tiny red and yellow fruit, where they once searched for green mantis. Even the fragrant noni, acacia, or hog apple trees, with their ripe yellow fruit hanging over the little canal, are missing here. But none of that matters. All they need is this muddy field, enough to light up the pages of their earliest memories.

Even though Thành and Minh were often scolded by Thành's mother for "roaming the streets all day," nothing brought them more joy than the annual mud-splashing event when the adults drained the pond beside the house to catch fish. The pond, situated between Thành and Minh's houses, was connected to a wide river branch, attracting fish and shrimp seeking refuge or a nesting place among the grass, bulrushes, and the nooks and crannies among the clusters of coconut and melaleuca roots along the pond's edge.

Nature had crafted this scene well, where, on ordinary days, birds chirped in the trees above while fish lazily swam below. After the pond was drained, the fish and shrimp, even half-hidden in the soft mud, were easily recognizable by their distinctive shapes: the long, sleek snakehead fish, the flat-headed catfish, the spiky climbing perch, or the gourami that looked like a mud-coated guava leaf. Each catch, big or small, brought joy to the adults and shouts of excitement from the children.

After the adults caught all the big fish, it was the children's turn to jump in and catch the smaller ones. Normally, muddy clothes and dirt-streaked hands and feet would earn them a scolding, but on pond-draining day, the kids were granted a special pass to dive into the mud to catch snails and tiny fish. Thành and Minh, however, had a secret mission of their own. Each took a side of the pond, searching for miniature fighting fish. On the muddy bed, these tiny fish looked like tamarind leaves covered in mud, recognizable only to keen eyes like Thành and Minh's, who would carefully catch them and place them in a basket.

Once on the bank, they'd bring the fish to the water jar behind the house, pouring in a few ladles of water to reveal their true colors. They selected the ones with vibrant blue-green or silvery scales, and if the fish had wide fins and a fan-like, purplish tail, it was even better. They placed these fish in a glass jar filled with water, adding a handful of soft, fresh green algae - for the fish to feed on, to hide in, and for people to admire.

Today, the two friends met again on a muddy field - not to search for fighting fish, but to catch crabs. It was a new game for Minh, but one Thành already knew well. Standing on the bank, Thành smiled as he watched Minh wade through ankle-deep mud, struggling to chase down every crab he spotted, whether it was wriggling by its burrow or scurrying around in search of food. Thành stepped forward confidently, ready to share his expertise:

"They're fast. You won't catch up just by chasing them."

Barely finishing his sentence, Thành spotted a crab darting ahead. He quickly tossed a handful of mud he had ready in his hand toward the crab. As it wriggled, trying to free itself from the clump of mud, Thành moved in, scooping it up into his hand and dropping it into his tin can.

After a few attempts, Minh thought he had mastered the art - learning both how to toss mud and how to block the crab's burrow to catch them. But at the end of the game, when they reached the bank and washed their crabs in the water jar, Minh realized the difference. The plain-looking crabs he'd caught were only fit for making shrimp paste. They couldn't compare to Thành's crabs, each with its own charm, flaunting red claws, green bodies, and even a hint of purple - making Minh a little envious.

Even the most joyful day must come to an end. After a long day playing in the muddy fields, the two friends returned to Thành's house. As they stepped into the front yard, Công's voice greeted them, urging:

"You two, wash up and come in to eat."

Thành led Minh to the side porch, pointing to a spot with a red-tiled floor beside a rainwater jar equipped with a dipping ladle, and said:

"You can bathe here."

Minh wasn't surprised. Just the day before, shortly after they arrived at the house, Công had changed into shorts and brought Minh to this very spot to pour a few ladles of water over himself to cool off.

What struck Minh as odd, however, was that Thành walked over to a different water jar near the mangrove trees by the canal bank to bathe alone. Minh reminisced about the past: after roaming the streets together, the two would often share a single water jar for their baths - sometimes at the side of Minh's house, and other times in Thành's backyard. Bathing at Thành's house always came with a playful tussle over the bigger ladle. Each of them wanted the larger ladle, which could pour more water at once and made the bath feel far more refreshing. The smaller ladle, originally a repurposed condensed milk can (Mr. Longevity brand), held only half the amount of water compared to the larger ladle, which was made from an old Guigoz milk can.

Minh had just splashed a few ladles of water over himself when Huệ, Thành's younger sister, appeared at the corner of the house. As usual, she was helping her mother by carrying pots and pans from the kitchen to the backyard to soak them in water for washing.

Suddenly, she froze, her eyes widening in surprise as she caught sight of Minh. Without a word, she quickly turned around and hurried back into the house. There was something in her expression and behavior that left Minh puzzled.

At first, Minh wondered if Huệ had been embarrassed to see him shirtless. But he immediately brushed off the thought—after all, not long ago, the three of them had run around together, carefree, playing in the rain on the streets. Huệ, still clad in her familiar *bà ba* outfit, would gleefully join in, while Minh and Thành wore nothing but their black shorts.

Huệ had often come up with playful games, like tossing her hair clip far away for the three of them to race and see who could retrieve it first. "Maybe she's grown up now and feels shy," Minh thought to himself briefly.

 After finishing their bath, Thành and Minh made their way into the house to change clothes. The family was already gathered around the dining table, waiting for the two of them. Thành's father was sipping his drink and, upon seeing Minh, sent a message for him to relay:

"Tomorrow, when you get back home, tell your father I said hello, okay?"

Minh replied with a polite "Yes," and Mr. Tám continued:

"Also, ask him how his *Cách* tree is doing these days. Just say that, and he'll know what I mean."

Minh understood Mr. Tám's intent. It was his way of fondly reminding Minh's father of the times they had enjoyed drinking together and feasting on beef wrapped in *Cách* leaves.

Thành's mother smiled warmly and said to Minh:

"Send my regards to your mom as well..."

She paused for a moment, took a bite of rice, and then added:

"Tell her I miss her so much. And ask her to let me know when she'll bring betel and areca nuts down here. I can't wait any longer."

Minh nodded, agreeing to pass on the message, though he didn't fully understand what Aunt Tám meant. After all, he was just a child, unaware of the deeper meanings behind adult conversations. The two women shared such a close bond that they had decided to solidify their friendship permanently by planning a future marriage between their children, Minh and Huệ, Thành's younger sister, once they came of age. Simply put, they had promised to become in-laws, with the boy's family bringing *betel and areca nuts* to the girl's house as part of the traditional marriage proposal ceremony.

Chapter 5: The Fresh Water Jar

'Every joyful moment passes quickly.'

The next morning, Minh bid farewell to Thành, his heart weighed down by the uncertainty of when they might meet again. As he sat on the bus near the Saltwater Canal ferry dock, he gazed at the rushing waters, which looked powerful enough to sweep away the Long Hựu islet. Suddenly, he recalled what Thành had mentioned the day before - that the canal had been dug by the French. Turning to Công, Minh asked,

"Brother, why did the French dig this canal?"

Công replied:

"They wanted to create a shortcut waterway from the Vàm Cỏ River to the Cần Giuộc River. It was a very strategic canal, convenient for their warships to travel and maintain control over the entire Southern region of Vietnam."

"So how did they travel before the canal?"

"I think their warships, if traveling from the Western region to Saigon, had to take a longer route along the Vàm Cỏ River to near the mouth of the Soài Rạp River before heading back upstream. Not only was it much farther, but they also had to face strong waves and winds near the river mouth. As the folk song goes:

'I took a rice boat from Gò Công,

To the estuary Bao Ngược, where storms tore the sails.'

(*Anh đi ghe gạo Gò Công / Về vàm Bao Ngược gió giông đứt buồm.*)

Estuary Bao Ngược is where the waters of the Vàm Cỏ River flow into the Soài Rạp River."

After pondering for a moment, Công continued:

"French warships departing from Mỹ Tho could also follow the Tiền River out to sea and then re-enter inland through the Soài Rạp estuary, which lies a bit further up. That route would have been even more distant and challenging."

Minh asked with curiosity,

"How did they know all the routes and paths in our land so well?"

Công let out a thoughtful 'hmm' before replying,

"They must have spent a lot of time exploring. It's likely the French authorities had sent ships here on earlier voyages under the guise of trade to scout the terrain."

"Were people really coming here for trade two or three hundred years ago?"

"Not just two or three hundred years ago. Traders from all over have been coming to this region for much longer."

"Really, brother?"

"Yes. During their time in Vietnam, the French discovered remnants of the Óc Eo culture, part of the ancient Funan (Phù

Nam) kingdom, which thrived nearly two thousand years ago in the Mekong Delta, especially around the An Giang region. There's even evidence that the people of Funan had trade relations with distant civilizations, possibly from other continents."

"That's fascinating, isn't it? I thought it was only around four or five hundred years ago, when the first Portuguese sailors circumnavigated the globe, that overseas foreigners might have first learned about us."

"That's based on historical records of official voyages commissioned by Western monarchs. But in reality, perhaps since the dawn of humanity, there's been the phenomenon of '*birds settling where the land is good.*' Whenever the fruit ran out or the wild game was scarce, people would instinctively move on to find another place to survive."

"So when did our people begin migrating to the Mekong Delta region?"

"Possibly around two thousand years ago, during the era of the Kingdom of Funan, there were Vietnamese drifting down here via sea or land routes. But according to historical records, the Nguyễn dynasty started establishing our southern borders in the late 17th century. During that time, the southern territories expanded thousands of miles, from east to west.

Minh asked curiously,

"Specifically, from where to where?"

Công gazed out through the glass window, smiled, and said:

"From:

'Nhà Bè, where the waters split in two.

Whoever goes to Gia Định or Đồng Nai, let them go.'

(Nhà Bè nước chảy chia hai / Ai về Gia Định, Đồng Nai thì về.)

To:

'Saigon lights, green and red.

Mỹ Tho lights, bright and dim.'"

(Đèn Sài Gòn ngọn xanh ngọn đỏ / Đèn Mỹ Tho ngọn tỏ ngọn lu.)

Công humorously mentioned the familiar landmarks that have become part of folklore, referencing the well-known southern provinces - from Đồng Nai (Biên Hòa) and Gia Định to Mỹ Tho - but he hadn't yet included other prominent provinces like Vĩnh Long, An Giang, and finally Hà Tiên.

After a moment of thought, Công continued:

"There's also a remarkable legacy from our ancestors that must not be overlooked:

'The route from Châu Đốc to Hà Tiên,

Connected by the Vĩnh Tế Canal.'

(Đường từ Châu Đốc, Hà Tiên / Có kinh Vĩnh Tế nối liền hai nơi.)

Minh asked curiously:

"Where is the Vĩnh Tế Canal, brother?"

Công nodded and explained:

"The Vĩnh Tế Canal was commissioned by King Gia Long, dug along our border with Cambodia. It served both as a strategic defense line and as a waterway to boost trade and development between the two nations."

Minh's eyes widened in admiration for the ingenuity of their forebears. Gazing out at the vast fields stretching beyond the window, Anh Công fell silent for a moment before reflecting:

"Those are the immediate benefits of the Vĩnh Tế Canal that later generations can see. But as for the deeper intentions of our ancestors, who could truly know?"

"Do you suppose King Gia Long had other purposes in mind when he ordered the excavation of the Vĩnh Tế Canal?"

"It's hard to say. Each era has its own context. The Vĩnh Tế Canal begins at the Châu Đốc River, connects to the Giang Thành River, flows through Hà Tiên, and empties into the Gulf of Thailand. Its obvious purpose was to promote trade between the Châu Đốc and Hà Tiên regions. It also helped attract the Khmer people to engage in commerce with us. Beyond that..."

Công trailed off, his thoughts steeped in admiration for the nation-building vision of their ancestors. After a moment of quiet reflection, he added in a hushed tone,

"In the past, our forefathers even marched as far as Phnom Penh to restore peace along the border, ensuring our people could live in safety. Imagine how much more efficient it would have been if the Vĩnh Tế Canal had existed back then, allowing the imperial court to swiftly deploy warships southward to quell unrest at the border."

Công pondered for a moment,

"If we look further, the Vĩnh Tế Canal wasn't just a route into Cambodia; it could also serve as a waterway extending all the way to Laos upstream - no small achievement."

Minh, captivated by Công's narrative, listened intently as if absorbing a priceless history lesson. Clicking his tongue in admiration, he asked,

"Our navy was that formidable? Able to sail from the central coast all the way here to quell uprisings?"

"Absolutely," Công replied. "Every time they reached a new location, after stabilizing the situation, the king would decree the construction of fortresses and assign skilled generals to defend them. It began with Gia Định Citadel, then Mỹ Tho Citadel, followed by Vĩnh Long Citadel, and so on. Step by step, this is how we solidified our sovereignty in the South."

Minh's excitement grew with each word,

"I had no idea we had such an invincible naval tradition!"

"Of course," Công replied. "More than a thousand years ago, Ngô Quyền defeated the Southern Han navy on the Bạch Đằng River, restoring our nation's independence. You've heard that in school, right? And over 300 years later, General Trần Quốc Tuấn, or Hưng Đạo Đại Vương, annihilated the Mongol invaders in naval battles. Not to mention the Battle of Hàm Tử, which Nguyễn Trãi proudly highlighted in his 'Proclamation of Victory over the Wu' (Bình Ngô đại cáo):

"… At Hàm Tử, Toa Đô was captured alive,

On the Bạch Đằng River, Ô Mã was slain."

(*Cửa Hàm tử bắt sống Toa Đô / Sông Bạch Đằng giết tươi Ô Mã.*)

Công pondered for a moment before continuing,

"But military strength and brute force alone aren't enough to build a nation or expand its borders. In our conflicts with powers large and small, from the North to the South, we've upheld a tradition:

'*Use righteousness to vanquish cruelty,*

Replace tyranny with compassion.'

(*Đem đại nghĩa để thắng hung tàn / Lấy chí nhân để thay cường bạo.*)

Minh asked curiously,

"Is that our secret?"

Công replied,

"You could say that. The secret lies in winning hearts and minds. Look at Genghis Khan, for example. He conquered vast territories, from East to West, from Asia to Europe, and from North to South, but everywhere he went, he left behind devastation, death, and deep resentment in people's hearts. In contrast, our ancestors, when reaching new lands with diverse and mixed populations, were able to unite people under a common cause."

"How did our ancestors win people's hearts?" Minh asked.

"They didn't have to do anything," Công replied.

"Why is that?" Minh asked, puzzled.

"Because running through our veins is a culture of kindness and good interpersonal relations."

"How do we know that?"

"The proof lies in the proverbs and folk sayings passed down through generations. Like, '*Love others as you love yourself,*' or '*O gourd, love the pumpkin though different you may be; for together you share a trellis tree.*'

('*Thương người như thể thương thân,*' hay '*Bầu ơi thương lấy bí cùng. Tuy rằng khác giống nhưng chung một giàn*'.)

Over time, they shaped our way of life, creating a natural warmth in our people. Who wouldn't feel at ease around us?"

Minh wondered aloud,

"What kinds of people lived in this area back then?"

After a moment of reflection, Công replied,

"As I mentioned, '*Good land attracts birds,*' right? The fertile Mekong Delta must have drawn people from all over - neighboring nations like Cambodia, Champa, and Siam, and even places farther away like India, China, Japan, and other island nations."

Minh's eyes widened with admiration,

"And they all ended up living among us today?"

Công nodded thoughtfully, attempting to explain,

"Each group that came here likely brought their own cultural traditions at first. Over time, they would have absorbed aspects of the local 'Óc Eo' culture that predated them. It shows how our culture needed to be flexible enough to create harmony in such a diverse society, yet robust enough to preserve our national identity to this day."

Minh didn't fully grasp Công's explanation, but he couldn't help feeling a swelling sense of pride and exhilaration for his homeland.

The bus rattled along, eventually rolling into Cần Giuộc, the halfway point on the journey back to Saigon, where it came to a halt to pick up more passengers. Outside, the sun blazed down mercilessly. Công raised his bag - filled with clothes and a few specialty gifts from the Saltwater Canal region - to the window to shield them from the harsh sunlight.

A handful of street vendors clustered around the bus, waving their hands energetically to catch the passengers' attention. Their persistence reminded Minh of the livelier and more bustling street vendor scenes near the Bến Lức Bridge, a familiar sight from his trips to his maternal grandparents' home in Long Xuyên. There, the air would be filled with the cacophony of vendors hawking their goods, their shouts mingling with the buzz of activity. Hands stretched eagerly toward the bus windows, offering an array of refreshments: skewers of freshly cut sugarcane, juicy slices of pineapple, or quick snacks like sausage-filled baguettes, skewered roasted sparrows, and steaming baskets of fertilized duck eggs.

As Minh let his thoughts wander to his maternal grandparents' home, he suddenly recalled Công mentioning An Giang as one of the Six Provinces of Southern Vietnam and asked,

"Earlier, you mentioned An Giang. That's where my grandparents live, right?"

"That's correct. Your hometown, Long Xuyên, is in An Giang Province. Although the borders and names of provinces in this region have shifted over time, your hometown is part of the Hậu River Delta, near the Ông Chưởng Islet area."

"I don't know who Ông Chưởng was, but I've noticed many temples dedicated to him in my hometown."

"Ông Chưởng was 'Lễ Thành Hầu Nguyễn Hữu Cảnh,' a brilliant general under Lord Nguyễn Phúc Chu. He made significant contributions to the southern expansion and is considered a pivotal figure in developing the An Giang region. People revered him and affectionately called him 'Chưởng Binh Lễ,' after his given title. After leading his troops as far as Phnom Penh to quell uprisings, he fell gravely ill upon returning to Cây Sao Islet, in the Hậu River near Long Xuyên, and passed away there. To honor his legacy, the locals renamed the islet 'Ông Chưởng Islet' and erected numerous temples across the region to worship him."

"He was amazing, wasn't he?" Minh said.

"Absolutely," Công replied. "Before that, he had already pacified two other Southern regions - Đồng Nai and Gia Định. He recruited settlers from Central Vietnam to reclaim the land, establish hamlets, and expand the frontier. While stationed in Gia Định, he received royal orders to lead his troops to the Cambodia border to suppress uprisings. Sadly, as I mentioned earlier, after his victory, he fell ill on his way back to An Giang and passed away."

The bus finally departed the station. As it crossed the Cần Giuộc Bridge, Công patted Minh on the shoulder and gestured toward the river below, saying,

"Look, there's a 'freshwater' boat."

Minh glanced down at the small, roofless cargo boat, which appeared almost submerged as it floated along the river.

"Why would anyone need to transport water in a place surrounded by rivers and streams?" Minh asked.

Công chuckled and explained,

"Rivers flow into the sea. No matter how 'fresh' the river water is upstream, by the time it gets near the coast, it becomes somewhat brackish."

"Like in your hometown?" Minh asked.

"Exactly," Công said. "And this year, there's been a drought - over a month without a single drop of rain. Many families can't even find clean freshwater to cook with and are left crying out in despair. Only the wealthier folks can afford to occasionally buy a load of freshwater brought in by boats from far away."

"Oh no, I stayed at your house for two days and didn't realize any of this."

Công put his arm around Minh's shoulder and said,

"Yesterday afternoon, while I was chatting with my parents at the dining table, little Huệ came running in, all flustered, shouting, 'Mom! Brother Minh is bathing with the rainwater!'"

"But I remember on the first day, you took me to that spot to rinse off."

"We were like 'guests' from far away, so the family made an exception. Besides, that day we had just returned from a long journey, so a quick splash or two to cool off was fine."

"But even Thành told me to bathe there."

"He values you, so he let you use the fresh rainwater. For himself, he would bathe with the brackish water first and only use a ladle or two of rainwater to rinse off. Freshwater is precious - it's reserved for drinking and cooking only."

Minh rubbed his head and neck, clenching his teeth to suppress the wave of guilt rising in his chest. The thought of wasting even a single ladle of the rare, precious drinking and cooking water of the salty-water region weighed heavily on him. Turning to Công, with red, tear-filled eyes, he whispered,

"I'm sorry, I didn't know..." Minh said.

Công ruffled Minh's hair and replied,

"Well, now you know. Life is a journey of learning."

After a moment of reflection, Công added,

"Even I didn't realize how hard life was for people in this region until my father moved us back here. When I was little and only visited my grandparents occasionally, I loved it. I'd spend entire days running through the fields with my cousins, then wash up from whichever water jar I fancied. The only time I ever felt regret was when we had to leave. I'd be so sad, almost in tears, and my grandfather would just laugh at me. My grandmother would try to cheer me up with promises: 'Next time you come, I'll make you plenty of toys.'"

How could Công ever forget the image of his grandmother sitting on her wooden bed, surrounded by green and yellow coconut leaves? She'd hunch over, squinting her eyes, and skillfully guide her thin, nimble fingers to weave creations - a grasshopper, a cricket, a dragonfly, or even a perch fish. Little Công would marvel, exclaiming, 'Grandma, you're amazing!' He'd admire how lifelike each creature looked. The grasshoppers and crickets always had their long, elegant antennae; the dragonflies never lacked their big, bulging eyes and long, delicate wings; and the perch fish gleamed with green and yellow 'scales.'

As for the coconut leaves, Công had heard that she had to ask a friend who sold goods by boat to bring them over from a neighboring village. And that wasn't all - she even knew how to make musical instruments. He still remembered one time, after preparing frog meat for a meal, she stretched the frog's skin over the mouth of an old condensed milk can and left it to dry, turning it into a drum for her grandson to play. Little Công spent the entire day happily beating that little drum with a chopstick, 'bung bung bung.'

How hard she worked, squeezing sweet, loving gifts out of the salty water and acidic soil for her grandchildren. Sitting on the bus back to the city, Công couldn't help but think of his grandmother with a deep fondness for his homeland. And Minh too - how could he ever forget Thành's generosity, offering his friend the rarest and most precious treasure of his village: a jar of freshwater for bathing?

Chapter 6: Life's Many Facets

The memory of that summer, when Minh reunited with his closest childhood friend, Thành, would likely remain with him forever. Yet, as he navigated the complexities of growing up, especially during those tumultuous days in a divided country struggling with the painful realities of war, Minh had no choice but to immerse himself in the relentless current of life.

In the summer of 1959, Minh took the entrance exam for Pétrus Ký Public High School in Saigon. Filling out the application form became an extended family affair, as they spent several days deliberating over one key issue: selecting Minh's primary foreign language course. The two options offered in high school were English and French. The primary language would be taught throughout all seven years, while the secondary language would only be introduced in the final three years of senior high school.

Minh personally preferred to continue studying French, having already built a foundation through elementary school lessons and private tutoring at home. However, his grandfather and father felt obligated to carefully weigh which foreign language would better serve Minh's future prospects.

Although Vietnam had gained independence from French rule four years earlier, French cultural influence and prestige remained deeply ingrained in society. This influence persisted even as

South Vietnam joined the free-world bloc led by the United States. Despite American aid trucks distributing second-hand clothing and canned goods in working-class neighborhoods, the arrival of U.S. advisors assisting with government reforms, and the first South Vietnamese president returning from the U.S. to assume office, French culture still held sway over the hearts and minds of many Vietnamese.

The perception that "speaking French sounds more sophisticated" and that French manners were "more elegant and refined" lingered, contrasting with the view that Americans were "boisterous and brash" with their cowboy-like demeanor. For many, French culture symbolized class and tradition, while American influence seemed foreign and unpolished.

Ultimately, Minh's family, like many others, chose to prioritize French over English, favoring the cultural prestige of the past over the practical considerations of the future.

In addition to the focus on choosing foreign languages, there was surprisingly little discussion about the structure of the Vietnamese language education program. During the French colonial period, only a small number of Vietnamese had access to schooling. Those who did were taught that *our ancestors were the Gauls,* as dictated by the colonial curriculum. Over time, however, the demand for civil servants to support the colonial administration, combined with growing pressure from the Vietnamese people, led to the increasing use of the written Vietnamese language in society - through books, newspapers, and eventually some schools.

Still, due to the French regime's policy of divide and rule and the distinct historical developments in each region, Vietnamese education programs evolved unevenly across the three regions of Vietnam. In the South, although pioneering scholars like Pétrus Trương Vĩnh Ký and Huỳnh Tịnh Của had made early contributions - such as publishing and editing 'Gia Định Báo', the first Vietnamese newspaper in 1865 - Vietnamese language education ultimately flourished more rapidly in the North.

The country's division in 1954 brought an unexpected silver lining to the South: it became home to many educators who migrated from the North. These educators played a crucial role in laying the foundation for the South's emerging education system. However, this migration also introduced a potential downside. Some have argued that Southern literature and the history of territorial expansion in the South may have been unintentionally overlooked or not given the attention they deserved.

While Minh and his peers grappled with choosing which foreign language courses to pursue in high school, their elders faced far more complex decisions about modernizing and building a democratic society in South Vietnam. Lacking historical precedents or homegrown political frameworks to bind and guide them in charting a course for the country - and amid constant interference by foreign powers seeking strategic alliances - numerous political and armed factions sprang up, squabbling and jostling for leadership. The result was constant disruption and turmoil throughout society.

Near Minh's house, there was a small roadside shop that served tea and coffee. In front of the shop, a couple of food stalls operated each morning - one selling '*cháo huyết*' (rice porridge with pork blood pudding) and the other '*cơm tấm*' (broken rice). Adults in the neighborhood often sent their children to buy breakfast and bring it home. In contrast, the taxi drivers preferred to eat on-site. They perched on tiny wooden stools, barely the size of an adult's foot, around low wooden tables set close to the ground. They would sip porridge while flipping through newspapers or enjoy broken rice while debating politics.

Uncle Năm leaned over and whispered something to Brother Tư, a taxi driver. A moment later, Brother Tư burst into boisterous laughter. Startled, a fellow driver sitting nearby asked,

"What's so funny, man?"

Brother Tư tilted his head back, glanced around, and then lowered his voice to repeat the verse he had just heard:

'*Sitting bored, scratching my crotch, the balls ripple.*'

"Who's in such high spirits?"

Brother Tư chuckled and whispered back,

"High spirits, my foot! I heard Mr. Hương wrote that poem while locked up in prison."

Brother Tư was referring to Mr. Trần Văn Hương, the former Mayor of Saigon and a well-known politician who had been imprisoned in Chí Hòa prison for his dissent against the ruling government. Hương, along with a group of intellectuals from various political factions, had formed an opposition against Ngô Đình Diệm's regime and openly supported the failed coup attempt of 1960.

In the early days of the Southern regime, while basic democratic institutions had been established, the fledgling political system - emerging after a prolonged period of instability under the colonial regime intertwined with feudalism - faced numerous challenges and opposition. Without precedent to guide its operation, the system often faltered. Many politicians and patriots found themselves repeatedly imprisoned. A notable example was scholar Hồ Hữu Tường, an intellectual and patriot whose life seemed inextricably linked to incarceration. Regardless of the era, he somehow always ended up behind bars. It became such a recurring pattern that people began to see it as his destiny. His name, Hữu Tường, was even humorously reinterpreted phonetically as '*hưởng tù*,' meaning 'enjoying prison' in Vietnamese.

Another profound social upheaval came with the arrival of American personnel and soldiers in South Vietnam - particularly the financial impact of the money they brought. At the height of the war, with half a million U.S. troops stationed there, the so-called green dollars and red dollars (special notes issued to soldiers by the U.S. government) poured into the economy. In a developing country, the almighty dollar, red or green, wielded immense power, reshaping the social and economic landscape.

Near the coffee shop, at the entrance of the alley beside Thành's house, there used to be a bustling food stall area that was lively from dawn till evening. Early each morning, Ms. Mẹo and her son could be seen bringing out baskets filled with 'bánh cam' (fried sesame balls) and 'bánh còng' (fried donut-like pastries) to sell to students and housewives on their way to the market. Next to Ms. Mẹo was Mrs. Sáu, celebrated in the neighborhood for her 'bánh ít trần' (sticky rice dumplings), known for their soft, tender dough, fragrant fillings, and perfectly balanced fish sauce. Beside Mrs. Sáu sat Ms. Hai, tending to a basket of 'xôi vò' (mung bean sticky rice), its enticing aroma of mung beans wafting through the air. Alongside the sticky rice, she showcased a bowl of nearly crystal-white 'cơm rượu' (fermented rice balls), exuding a rich, sweet fragrance of rice and fermentation that drew in passersby.

Every afternoon, if Ms. Mẹo couldn't sell all her pastries, she would signal her son, Tươi, to go around the neighborhood hawking them door-to-door. Sometimes, he would approach the men playing "bools" (the local name for pétanque, a colonial-era game introduced by the French) in the alley. Although the French were no longer in Vietnam, Khmer and Vietnamese soldiers still gathered there to play bools. They didn't play for leisure but for money, and the winner, often pleased with their victory, would buy Ms. Mẹo's pastries to share with friends.

The alley's entrance remained lively well into the evening and night. Pedestrians walking near the streetlight at the alley's entrance could already catch the aroma of grilled squid. Closer inspection would reveal flattened yet plump grilled bananas and golden roasted corn laid out on a wire rack atop tin boxes filled with glowing charcoal. Beside them, a bowl of fragrant green onion oil added to the allure, enticing passersby to stop and indulge.

This afternoon, during a lull in customers, Ms. Hai noticed their familiar neighbor walking past the alley. She called out to Mrs. Sáu:

"Mrs. Sáu, did you know he's running schemes for the Americans?"

"Yeah, I've heard people say that, but I don't really know what kind of work he's doing."

Ms. Hai, trying to sound informed, continued:

"I heard he's got a lot of connections with the Americans and is making big money."

"Now that you mention it, I remember hearing about someone who got a contract to clean and collect trash for the American offices and ended up making a fortune."

"We should ask him one day to help us find some easy work like that. Then we wouldn't have to stay up late or wake up early to make sticky rice and pastries for such little profit."

"But how could we work for them when we don't even speak their language?"

"Look at Lành from our neighborhood. She doesn't know a single word of English, and yet she's working for the Americans."

"Yeah, but I heard from Lành the other day that the Americans are really stingy. It's not easy to get money out of them."

"Really? How stingy are they, Mrs. Sáu?"

"She said those Americans don't even eat a whole mango. They just cut off one piece to eat and put the other half in the fridge to save for the next day. How stingy can they be, seriously?"

"Oh, stop it, Mrs. Sáu. They've got piles of dollars - enough to burn both you and me, and it wouldn't even matter. Stingy? No way."

Mrs. Bảy, a regular customer who was sitting nearby eating 'bánh ít trần' (sticky rice dumplings), overheard the conversation and chimed in:

"Ms. Hai is right, Mrs. Sáu. Those Americans are filthy rich. They treat money like it's nothing."

Mrs. Sáu raised her eyebrows in surprise:

"Really?"

Mrs. Bảy set her plate down and added:

"Last New Year, I had a niece selling goods in front of Saigon Market. She said the Americans spend lavishly."

"Is that so?"

Mrs. Bảy nodded enthusiastically, her eyes widening as she looked at Mrs. Sáu:

"You know what? They don't even haggle when they buy stuff. And if something's packaged in a bag, they'll buy the whole bag instead of just picking one or two pieces."

Mrs. Sáu widened her eyes in surprise, waiting expectantly. Mrs. Bảy picked up her plate of dumplings, scooped up the last bits of mung bean filling, and tilted her head back to slurp the sweet-and-sour garlic chili fish sauce before exclaiming:

"Goodness, they even buy handkerchiefs by the dozen, Mrs. Sáu! Right after buying them, they tear open the bag right there, pull out two or three handkerchiefs to wipe their sweat, and then throw them straight into the trash. My niece saw that and couldn't help but feel bad about the waste."

"Who wouldn't feel bad about that? replied Mrs. Sáu, reaching for the plate and placing it in the wash water."

Mrs. Bảy stood up, grabbed her basket, and left for the evening market. Ms. Hai, who sold 'xôi vò' (mung bean sticky rice), held a piece of banana leaf in her hand as she served a portion to Tốt, the water carrier, to take home to her younger sibling waiting at home. Everyone went about their business, each absorbed in their own tasks. Meanwhile, Ms. Mẹo sat counting the few piasters she had earned for the day, over and over again, before carefully tucking them into the pocket of her blouse and securing it with a pin. She was saving every penny she could, hoping to one day afford surgery to repair her son's cleft lip.

Ms. Mẹo had lost her voice at the age of ten, supposedly because of eating watermelon - or so her parents used to say. Shortly before the New Year that fateful year, she had survived a severe illness, though her voice remained hoarse. But after eating a few sliccs of watcrmelon during the festive season, her voice suddenly disappeared completely. From that point on, misfortunes seemed to shadow her life. A few years later, her parents passed away, one after the other. Left with no choice, she became a maid for a French family.

After the Geneva Accords were signed, ending French colonial rule in Indochina, the family's wife and two children left for France first. The husband stayed behind for another month to complete his administrative duties during the transition. Then, one night, he unleashed all his pent-up anger and humiliation over his country's defeat onto Ms. Mẹo.

When little Tươi was born, Ms. Mẹo watched in anguish as she noticed her child's lips were not like those of other children. His lip was split in two at the philtrum. The French departure had left Ms. Mẹo with a child born with a cleft lip and left the Vietnamese people with a divided country and fractured hearts.

In South Vietnam, after the government eradicated the remnants of armed criminal groups that had thrived under colonial rule and stabilized the situation, the light of peace began to shine, breaking through what once seemed like an endless storm. Yet, that light was fleeting, as dark clouds soon gathered once more.

In early 1962, Minh was in eighth grade at Pétrus Ký High School, a prestigious public school in Saigon with a strong anti-French legacy. One February morning, Minh and his classmates were milling around outside the school gate, waiting for it to open. Suddenly, the distant sounds of explosions and machine gun fire broke the calm.

Some sharp-eyed students pointed to the sky ahead of the school and shouted, "Planes are bombing!" Minh looked up to see two airplanes circling, weaving in and out of sight behind clusters of clouds. One student speculated,

"They're probably bombing Nhà Bè."

Another added,

"Maybe there's a clash in the Rừng Sát forest."

When the gates finally opened, the students filed into the schoolyard in an orderly manner and lined up for class as usual, unaware that they had just witnessed a bombing targeting the center of power in South Vietnam - the Presidential Palace, less than three kilometers away. The event occurred a little over a year after a failed coup attempt by military officers, marking yet another sign of the instability foreshadowing the turbulent days ahead.

The political situation may have been unstable, and the war was dragging on, but the wheels of the economy kept turning, thanks largely to people's ingenuity and hard work, coupled significantly with the influx of dollars from U.S. aid and spending by U.S. personnel in Vietnam. This economic vitality created opportunities that were simply too enticing for many to ignore.

Ba Đơ, the younger brother of Hai On, stood out as a particularly memorable figure who carved out a unique niche in this war-fueled economy. Born to a wealthy landowner from Cái Bè, he was sent to Saigon by his family to pursue an education. However, Ba Đơ spent far more time learning from the streets than from the classroom, and by the age of thirty-five, he had established himself as a prominent dealmaker in the capital.

Wherever Ba Đơ went, he left a vivid impression, always dressed in dazzling white. Stepping out of his white Simca convertible, he sported a full tennis ensemble: a crisp white polo shirt tucked into white shorts, paired with spotless white sneakers and knee-high white socks - perhaps an attempt to compensate for his short legs. The only element disrupting his carefully curated image was his deeply tanned skin. On his thick, calloused left hand gleamed a massive Siamese diamond ring, so large it seemed capable of knocking out a dog if thrown. No matter where he appeared, Ba Đơ was never without the latest issue of 'Playboy', the glossy magazine featuring nude photos, which he clutched as if it were his most prized possession.

If "A betel quid starts the conversation," as the Vietnamese proverb goes, then the "betel quid" Ba Đơ served his guests was none other than the latest nude images from a popular American men's magazine. The stories he told, however, were tailored to whatever his clients needed to hear. Well-connected with influential figures, he knew every bureaucratic loophole, every shortcut, and every backdoor to resolve even the most complicated dilemmas his clients faced. His words often reassured his listeners, leaving them nodding gratefully and repeatedly saying, almost like a mantra, "A hundred things depend on you, Sir." After parting with him, they would walk away with a lighter spirit, as if a thousand-pound burden had been lifted from their weary shoulders.

As the war escalated, so did Ba Đo's clientele. More and more people sought his help to obtain "deferment papers" for their children to escape military conscription. The army's need for troops made drafting young men a common practice. Yet not everyone joined reluctantly; young men enlisted for a variety of reasons - some out of idealism, others out of necessity, and still others inspired by the romanticized image of a soldier. A clear example of this was Thọ's brothers, Minh's schoolmates and neighbors. Since Thọ's older brother had joined the prestigious military academy in Đà Lạt, Thọ openly shared with his friends his dream of passing the second baccalaureate exam and following in his brother's footsteps.

The image of the soldier that Thọ and his brother first encountered and deeply admired was that of the red-beret paratroopers pursuing Bình Xuyên rebels in the area near their house. Before the skirmish, Thọ and his brother had been hiding inside their home, observing from the entrance of an alley adjacent to their wall. There, they spotted a soldier lying prone on the street, gripping a machine gun in a ready position, prepared to face any enemy that might charge out of the alley.

Fortunately for the entire neighborhood, after a night of intense fighting near the riverbank, the enemy was forced to retreat across the river, fleeing back to their stronghold in Rừng Sát. Early the next morning, the victorious paratroopers returned, gathering on the street in front of Thọ's house. The townspeople, overjoyed, poured into the streets to welcome their heroes. Thọ's father climbed a tree to gather coconuts to offer the soldiers. Neighbors, too, shared whatever they could - some brought plums, others guavas, presenting baskets of fruit to the troops as heartfelt gestures of gratitude.

Thọ admired and respected the soldiers even more for their sense of discipline. Initially, they politely declined the gifts offered by the townsfolk. It wasn't until their commanding officer, a young and dignified lieutenant, arrived and expressed his gratitude to the people that the soldiers began to interact with the local residents, engaging in friendly conversations and cheerfully accepting the refreshing fruits offered to them.

Not every young man growing up during wartime was like Thọ and his brother. Many sought ways to evade military service, creating opportunities for people like Ba Đơ. Depending on the financial means of the young men's parents - often desperate to keep their sons out of the draft - Ba Đơ would provide a tailored solution. While Sun Tzu's 'The Art of War' is said to include 36 strategies, Ba Đơ always managed to devise the 37th, 38th, and countless other "miracles." For example, if someone wished to defer military service, he knew of a temple where the young man could temporarily ordain as a monk, and he would "arrange" the necessary paperwork to secure an exemption on religious grounds.

Ba Đơ could also "arrange" exemption papers for family hardship reasons, such as claiming the young man was the only son of a widowed mother, even if both his parents were alive, well, and wealthy enough to afford Ba Đơ's services. In more extreme cases, he could secure a certificate declaring the young man a "reformed defector" - someone who had supposedly fought on the opposing side but had returned to support the government under the reconciliation program (Chiêu Hồi). This method was risky: if it worked, the young man would be exempt from service; if it failed, he could easily end up in jail.

Though Ba Đơ had been quite busy recently managing exemption requests, he still juggled other business opportunities. That afternoon, he received a call from a wealthy client looking for help securing a contract to provide civilian services to an American military camp being built on the outskirts of town. Ba Đơ stepped out to the alley where he parked his car during the day, preferring it over maneuvering in and out of his cramped driveway. Parking on the street had its downsides - kids in the neighborhood might mess with his car - so he usually paid the "cleft-lip boy," the son of the mute woman who sold fried snacks on the roadside, to keep watch over it.

The boy, Tươi, and his mother, Mrs. Mẹo, lived in the alley behind Ba Đơ's house, but he neither knew their names nor cared to. As he passed by Tươi sitting next to his mother, Ba Đơ silently handed the boy a one-piaster bill and continued toward his car. He started the engine and drove off, leaving behind a cloud of dust in the narrow alley.

The client of Ba Đơ, a middle-aged man with hair slicked back with Brillantine gel - smooth, shiny, and combed straight back - sat waiting for him at a blood pudding shop across from the Nguyễn Văn Hảo theater. The man, wearing a shirt adorned with bird and crane patterns, looked up as Ba Đơ parked his vehicle by the roadside. Without delay, Ba Đơ hurried over, warmly greeting the man with enthusiastic handshakes and a broad smile, as if reuniting with an old, dear friend. Bending low, Ba Đơ extended both hands to clasp the client's hands.

"Brother Hai, you're still well and making good money, I hope?" Ba Đơ greeted.

Mr. Hai chuckled, "Whether I make money or not depends on you."

Ba Đơ waved his hands in mock humility. "Oh no, no, I wouldn't dare take the credit."

As he spoke, Ba Đơ glanced around conspiratorially, giving the impression that he held a secret too sensitive to share openly. Then, with an air of nonchalance, he let slip a glimpse of a shiny silver object in his hand. Mr. Hai's eyes widened as he immediately recognized it - a small pistol, the kind he had only ever seen wielded by female spies in films. Breaking into a cold sweat, he cast a quick, nervous glance around to ensure no one else had noticed.

"Put it away," he hissed urgently.

Mr. Hai, ever the cautious businessman who valued profits over problems, watched uneasily as Ba Đơ puffed up his chest and slipped the "gun" into his pants pocket. Lowering his voice, Mr. Hai asked, "CIA, huh?"

By this, he meant to inquire if Ba Đơ was working for the American intelligence agency, the CIA, and had received the weapon through such connections. Sensing the bait had been swallowed, Ba Đơ put on an air of mystery, pressing his lips together as if sworn to secrecy. He darted his eyes around theatrically before casually redirecting the conversation.

"I wonder what's playing at the theater today," Ba Đơ remarked with feigned curiosity.

Mr. Hai ordered a plate of blood pudding, plenty of boiled innards, and two bottles of beer before getting to the point.

"I heard from some folks in the district near my house that the Americans are planning to fill in the water spinach pond owned by Northern migrants from back in the day, maybe to build an army supply warehouse or something."

"I already know."

"Oh, that's great. If there's any good contracting opportunities, please let me know."

"Alright, leave it to me."

"That's great. With you handling it, I feel confident."

Ba Đơ hesitated, as if there was something difficult to say.

“This job might require some bucks, you know.”

What job doesn't need money? He never worked for free for anyone. But Mr. Hai understood what he meant.

“That's not an issue. Doing business requires building relationships. Just let me know how much you need upfront.”

“I'm just saying so you can prepare, but any day works.”

“Alright then, whenever you need it, just come by my office. I'll always be there.”

Saying goodbye to Mr. Hai, Ba Đơ got into his car, glancing around cautiously before pulling out his lighter to light a cigarette. Had Mr. Hai seen it, he would have been quite surprised - the "spy gun" he imagined Ba Đơ carried was, in truth, just a lighter Ba Đơ had pleaded and bargained to buy from a friend two days prior. Taking a few puffs to clear his head, Ba Đơ started the car and drove straight to Cercle Sportif.

The Cercle Sportif sports club, complete with its tennis courts, had once been the exclusive domain of French colonial elites. Now, it served as the playground of the new masters of the land - among them, the 'nouveau riche' ("new rich"), a French term borrowed by American media to vividly characterize an era ruled by the omnipresent power of American red and green dollars.

Ba Đơ arrived to meet his contact - one of those he believed had direct "connections to the sun." In truth, they were only close associates of those who were close associates of the "sun." Some might even be distant relatives of the household confidants of an enigmatic power broker who could command storms with a whisper.

Ba Đơ walked directly to the refreshment table at the end of the hallway, shaded by the flamboyant tree. As always, his "partner" was seated there, dressed in a crisp white shirt and sunglasses, casually reading a newspaper. Despite working together for three years - introduced by another associate - Ba Đơ still didn't know where the man lived or even have his phone number. Their meetings were brief, just long enough to arrange a plan before heading to a pub or restaurant, either in the city or further afield, depending on the size of the business deal.

This time, Ba Đơ felt the occasion warranted a more generous gesture. He suggested,

"Today, Brother Tư, if you don't mind, let me treat you to grilled lobster at Bình Điền Bar."

Bình Điền, located about 20 kilometers south of Saigon on the road to the Mekong Delta, was renowned for its pub nestled in a stilt house surrounded by rice fields. Out on the wooden deck in front, several outdoor dining tables were arranged, offering a tranquil ambiance. At night, diners could enjoy their meals under the moonlight and cool breeze. However, stargazing was often hindered by the dazzling glow of red and green lights from colorful bulbs strung across the tangled wires overhead. For many, the vibrant atmosphere added charm to the experience, and they appreciated the pub owner's foresight in installing a private generator to bring the "light of civilization" to this rural idyll.

It had been a long time since Mr. Tư had ventured out of the city, and the mention of grilled lobster did pique his interest. However, given the recent unrest in the countryside, he was cautious about drinking too much, losing track of time, and finding himself stuck in the suburbs at night. He tactfully replied,

"Why go all the way out there just for lobster? Saigon has plenty of places for that."

Ba Đơ misunderstood, thinking Mr. Tư wasn't keen on lobster, and quickly proposed,

"Then how about some roasted veal, boss? Wrapped in rice paper and dipped in 'mắm nêm' sauce - nothing compares!"

Mr. Tư glanced outside, noticing the twilight settling in, and suggested,
"Speaking of veal, why don't we just go to Pagolac in Chợ Lớn for a simple seven-course beef meal and call it a night?"

Ba Đơ, however, felt that place was too modest and worried it wouldn't match the grandeur of the million-dollar deal he was brokering. He countered enthusiastically,

"If you're up for a little drive, how about we head to Biên Hòa for some steamed fish head instead?"

Mr. Hai considered it and found no objections. The restaurant in Biên Hòa that Ba Đơ suggested, though located in another city, seemed more secure. They got into Ba Đơ's car and drove to the restaurant. After a few rounds of drinks and finishing two steamed fish heads, they strolled around the restaurant's grounds - by the riverbank, along the pond, under the coconut trees. In the shadows, they shook hands and sealed an agreement to act as intermediaries for a service that promised substantial profits for all parties involved.

Ba Đo's booming business mirrored the escalation of the war and the expanding American presence in Vietnam, which brought about deeper U.S. interference in South Vietnam's politics. On November 1, 1963, after three days of student demonstrations in support of protests against the government's handling of the Buddhist crisis, the military launched a coup and overthrew the administration. American newspapers featured headlines such as "Coup d'état in Saigon," employing the French term commonly used by U.S. media to describe the violent overthrow of a government, whether directly or indirectly orchestrated by the military. To justify their actions, the military framed it as a "revolution."

The morning after the revolution, at some schools, students were still swept up in the fervor of "taking to the streets," gathering in front of schoolyards and refusing to go to class. In the front yard of Pétrus Ký School, students surrounded an armored military vehicle stationed there since the previous day, chatting with the soldiers, ignoring the Principal's attempts to call them into class using a loudspeaker.

Everything only changed when the commanding lieutenant made an announcement. He climbed atop the tank with a megaphone in hand and boldly addressed the students:

"Do you love the revolution?"

The students below enthusiastically shouted back,

"Yes!"

"Do you love the military?"

"Yes!"

"Then do you listen to the military?"

This time, the response of "Yes" was much weaker because, despite their reputation for being mischievous troublemakers, the students realized they were caught in a logical trap. The lieutenant continued his gentle persuasion:

"If that's the case, then please go back to your classes and restore order so that the soldiers can return to their unit. They've been working hard for two days now."

That was all it took for the mischievous group to reluctantly shuffle back to their classrooms.

In Minh's class, the literature teacher nodded thoughtfully as he explained to the students how they had been caught by the "syllogism" used by the armored corps officer. Minh couldn't help but wonder what was going through his teacher's mind at that moment. The teacher, one of the older instructors from Quảng Nam Province, had once been deeply devoted to the now-deposed President. He had even written poetry in honor of the former leader, which he often recited to his students:

"The patriot departed that day,

The land still aflame with the fires of war..."

(*Người chí sĩ ra đi từ dạo ấy / Nước non còn bừng lửa binh đao...*)

These lines evoked the time when "The Patriot" (now the deposed president) resigned from his post in the Nguyễn Dynasty under French rule and journeyed abroad in search of a way to save the nation.

Minh couldn't help but feel a twinge of sadness as he recalled the pride in his teacher's voice whenever he recounted meeting the President during one of the leader's provincial visits. The teacher would solemnly describe those honored moments of his life, pointing at two student desks positioned close to each other and saying, "The President sat here, and I sat here."

In recent days, however, the teacher often came to class slightly intoxicated, somber and withdrawn, speaking little except to fulfill his duty of delivering lessons. His air of disillusionment reminded Minh of the melancholic verses by Nguyễn Khuyến that the teacher had once taught:

"When inspired, drink a few more cups of wine,

When sad, recite a line of poetry in vain."

(*Lúc hứng uống thêm dăm chén rượu / Khi buồn ngâm láo một vần thơ.*)

It was, perhaps, an early lesson in life's realities for his students - a lesson about the fragility of hollow fame and the fickle nature of human loyalties in politics. Publicly, people shouted praises, but privately, they schemed to pull the throne out from under him.

It was reminiscent of Nguyễn Công Trứ's lament in *"Meditation on Life"*:

> *"Looking back on all that's come and gone, one cannot help but feel dismayed;*
>
> *Life's treachery resembles a sleight of hand."*

(Những nghĩ xa gần khéo gớm thay / Sự đời tráo trở giống bàn tay.)

Chapter 7: The Moment of Separation

'Heartbreaking is the moment of separation.'[1]

It had been three years since Minh last saw Thành. During that time, the only news he received came from Thành's older brother, Công, who occasionally visited Minh's family. But even those updates stopped when Công was drafted into the military, joining the 13th class of the Thủ Đức Reserve Officers School in 1962.

The most recent information Minh had heard was that, after completing elementary school in the Saltwater Canal Hamlet, Thành had moved to a nearby provincial town to continue his studies at Cần Đước High School, boarding with an aunt.

On this Sunday afternoon, as had become his routine in recent months, Minh headed to the backyard around 3 o'clock to lift weights. It wasn't a habit he had developed out of passion, but rather one imposed by his father's firm encouragement: "You're as scrawny as a fiddler crab. How are you going to carry a gun when you join the army?"

Previously, when Minh used to work out with Hòa, a close friend who lived nearby, he had been more disciplined, training three times a week on a rotating schedule: Monday-Wednesday-Friday one week, and Tuesday-Thursday-Saturday the next. Hòa had a

---

[1] A rendition of the line *'Đoạn trường thay lúc phân kỳ'* from Nguyễn Du's 'The Tale of Kiều'.

professional-grade weightlifting set, a gift sent by his older brother studying in France. Their workout area was a spacious cement yard situated between the front villa and two rear annexes. One annex housed the kitchen, while the other served as a storage space for gardening tools and Hòa's sports equipment.

Before each session, the two of them would carry out the weightlifting bench and equipment, setting everything up in the yard. After an hour-long workout, they would pack it all back into storage. Minh's favorite part of these sessions was the relaxation afterward, when Hòa would lead him on a stroll through the fruit garden surrounding the villa in search of something to eat.

There was sugarcane - a whole cluster growing in the corner by the fence - that they could chop down, peel, and chew to their hearts' content. Two plum trees, heavy with fruit, offered an endless supply for picking. The mango tree, with its lush canopy casting cool shade over one corner of the garden, bore clusters of hanging green mangoes. They would pick some, slice them thin, and dip the slices into a mix of fish sauce and sugar for a tangy-sweet treat. There was even a custard apple tree, its fruits nearly the size of grapefruits. However, those weren't for eating; they were reserved for display or offerings. Instead, Minh and Hòa would content themselves with just admiring or lightly sniffing the fragrant fruit to satisfy their cravings.

This was heaven, in Minh's eyes. After just a few sets of lifting those iron weights, his muscles were already tightening, and he felt as if he could hold up the sky with one hand. His heart soared as if stepping into paradise itself, ready to revel in the essence of earth and sky.

Alas, harsh reality has a way of creeping in unnoticed. After the workout, as Minh squeezed his bike through the slightly ajar iron gates in front of Hòa's house, the hell of the mortal world came crashing down. The towering yellow wall of the old French tax office loomed across the street, its imposing presence shrouding the secrets inside. Just thinking about it sent chills down Minh's spine.

The two-story building by the riverside was originally constructed by the French colonial government as a tax collection facility. Boats carrying grain, livestock, and fruit from farmers in the Mekong Delta were stopped there to pay taxes before being allowed to enter the city and distribute their goods to wholesalers across Saigon. However, since the French departed Vietnam a decade ago, they were no longer there to extract the sweat and toil of the farmers.

As for the building's current owners or its purpose - whether it was government-controlled or not - no one knew for certain. Some speculated that it had been repurposed as a new base for the special police force, established by the current Vietnamese regime to target opposition parties and anti-government activists.

However, some believed it was the headquarters of the 'Secret Service.' But what exactly did they do? Matters of secrecy and national affairs, no doubt - how could Minh possibly know? Still, he vaguely understood it to mean people working covertly for the government or an agency operating in the shadows to ensure the regime's security. Those who claimed to be informed likened it to an octopus with countless tentacles, reaching into every corner of society. Its presence seemed to loom even in the most remote and hidden places.

After the coup overthrowing the government in 1963, Minh's classmates whispered among themselves that the "two older men" who used to sit at the back of the class were gone. This referred to two new students who had appeared suddenly and looked much older than the rest of the class. In earlier years, during Minh's lower grades, they were nowhere to be seen. Then, one year, they arrived unexpectedly, sitting quietly at the back of the room. Just as abruptly, they vanished. "They're Secret Service agents," Minh's friends speculated. There was even a teacher who often wore sunglasses to school, and students whispered, "He's with the Secret Service."

Whether the yellow wall of the old tax office now hides 'police' or 'secret agents' behind it makes little difference. Pedestrians instinctively cross to the other side of the street, lower their heads, shield their faces, and hurry past like thieves avoiding prying eyes. Only once they've put some distance behind them do they remember to breathe. Cyclists like Minh keep their eyes fixed straight ahead, careful not to pedal too fast or too slow, wary of drawing attention. They grit their teeth and maintain a steady pace until they've passed those yellow-painted walls.

After Hòa enlisted in the army, Minh's father crafted homemade weights for him to train with at home. His improvised equipment was made from a wooden carrying pole. Unlike the traditional shoulder pole, which is flat and flexible, the carrying pole is round and rigid, with its ends sometimes sharpened to pierce bundles of rice for lifting or carrying. Transforming the pole into exercise weights was simple: Minh's father filled two empty fish sauce jars with a mixture of sand and cement, then secured them to either end of the pole. After letting the cement dry for a few days, the weights were ready. Lifting the pole up and down would feel like real weightlifting, with a solid 10 kilograms or more in hand.

Minh was lifting weights in the backyard when he heard his mother, Mrs. Hai, called out urgently,

"Minh, come up here! Someone's here to see you!"

Minh's first thought was of Hòa, but the joyful surprise in his mother's voice hinted that it might be someone else - someone he hadn't seen as often. Pulling back the curtain to step into the front room, Minh stopped short. Before him stood two young women in pristine white 'áo dài', the elegant traditional uniform worn by high school girls. They nodded politely in greeting. Minh returned the gesture, but their faces didn't ring a bell.

Mrs. Hai was half-hidden beside the family altar cabinet, flipping through an old photo album as she showed Thành some childhood pictures. She looked amazed at how much he had changed.

Overcome with excitement at the unexpected reunion, Minh burst out,

"Thành!"

Thành turned around, and Minh was taken aback - his friend now stood nearly a head taller, his skin bronzed from years under the sun. With a faint smirk, Thành said,

"Minh, it's been a while, hasn't it?"

"Yeah, since that summer at your place in Saltwater Canal Hamlet, when we went crab-catching together."

Minh then glanced curiously at the two young women, and Thành, noticing his look, introduced them,

"This is Hồng, and this is Thu. My classmates."

Mrs. Hai, ever tactful, smiled and said,

"It's so hot today; I'll go out back and ask the kids to pick some coconuts for you all to drink."

Though Minh had often thought of his friend, Thành's sudden appearance today, accompanied by two unfamiliar girls, left him feeling awkward and unsure of how to respond. Thành walked over, patted Minh on the shoulder, and asked,

"Is the temple still the same as before?"

Minh was caught off guard by the question, wondering why Thành was suddenly asking about the temple across the street. Assuming that Thành was reminiscing about their childhood adventures picking rose apples there, Minh replied,

"The rose apple tree is still there, but it doesn't seem to bear as much fruit as it used to."

Thành's expression remained indifferent. Minh, remembering something, added,

"Oh, Mr. Tạ, the caretaker who used to open the gate for us to pick rose apples, passed away last year."

Thành glanced at the two young women, then back at Minh, and said casually,

"Really?"

Minh, unsure of what to say next, noticed Hồng fanning herself with her handbag and suggested,

"Why don't we sit out on the front veranda? There's a nice breeze out there."

Thành quickly pointed to a small guest table near the wall and said,

"No, let's just sit here."

As soon as they sat down, Minh noticed Thành glancing at his watch and asked,

"Do you have to go somewhere?"

In Minh's mind, Thành might be worried about missing the afternoon bus back to Cần Đước, where, as far as Minh knew, Thành was staying with his aunt to continue his high school studies. Thành shook his head, hesitated as if searching for the right words, but before he could respond, Minh asked again,

"Are you worried about missing the bus?"

Thành looked momentarily surprised, then quickly replied,

"I biked here."

Minh grew even more puzzled,

"I thought you were studying in Cần Đước?"

Thành glanced at Hồng and Thu, hesitated for a moment, and lowered his voice,

"I moved up here this school term."

"Where are you studying?"

"Trần Hưng Đạo."

"Trần Hưng Đạo High School?"

"Yeah."

Minh couldn't help but wonder why Thành, despite being in the same city, hadn't visited him or his family in over a month. After a moment of contemplation, he asked,

"So, where are you staying?"

Thành hesitated before replying,

"At my grandaunt's house."

"Which grandaunt? I've never heard of her," Minh said, puzzled.

Thành glanced briefly at Hồng and Thu, then reluctantly explained,

"She's one of my grandfather's cousins from way back, down in the countryside."

Minh continued to probe,

"Where does your grandaunt live?"

"In Xóm Chiếu," Thành answered curtly.

The more Minh inquired, the more baffled he felt. They had always been as close as brothers, yet it seemed there was so much about Thành that Minh had never known.

Just then, four glasses of coconut water were set on the table. Minh politely offered them to Hồng and Thu, but Thành quickly interjected with a suggestion,

"Let's head over to the temple once we're done here."

Minh hadn't even had a chance to respond when Thành threw an arm around his shoulder, just like old times, and said,

"You'll be our guide, alright?"

Minh raised an eyebrow, finding it strange.

"You know every corner of the temple as well as I do."

"Sure, but it's been years. I'm not even sure if anyone there still remembers me."

Minh glanced at the two girls sitting quietly nearby. Their distant gazes frequently wandered outside, showing little interest in visiting the temple. Attempting to start a conversation, Minh asked,

"You two study at the same school as Thành?"

The girls nodded softly. Minh, still curious, continued,

"Where are you two from?"

Before they could reply, Thành abruptly set his glass of coconut water down, stood up, and urged,

"Come on, let's head to the temple before it closes."

Minh gave him a surprised look,

"Did you forget? The temple doesn't close until six."

By then, the two girls had already risen and stood beside Thành. Seeing this, Minh smiled and stepped outside, happily taking on the role of their guide.

As soon as they stepped through the temple gate, Minh pointed to the rose apple tree partially blocking the entrance to the Buddhist School building and enthusiastically shared with Hồng and Thu the 'legendary' stories associated with the tree from his and Thành's childhood. The two girls politely listened before expressing their interest in exploring the temple grounds. Minh eagerly led the way, but when he glanced back, Thành was nowhere to be seen. Scanning the area, Minh spotted Thành standing in front of a young monk's quarter, deep in conversation with the monk. Minh found it puzzling - how could Thành know him, given that the monk had only recently been ordained? It was also unusual for monks to entertain visitors at their quarters. Thinking that Thành must be well-acquainted with the temple, Minh carried on, guiding the two girls to the main hall and then circling to the back courtyard to visit the "Ascetic Statue," as it was commonly called by the locals.

A while later, Thành reappeared, and after briefly thanking Minh, he and the two girls said their goodbyes and left. Minh wandered back home, feeling disheartened by how unexpectedly dull the reunion with Thành had been. When Minh recounted Thành's and his friends' departure to Mrs. Hai, she chided him for not inviting them to stay for dinner.

The following afternoon, Mrs. Hai and two neighborhood women were sitting on the wooden divan by the side of the house, waiting for a fourth player to start a game of 'Tứ sắc' (Four-color card game, popular among the elderly). During a time of strict crackdowns on gambling, even small, friendly games at home could attract unwanted attention from the authorities. But things were different at Minh's house. Minh's family, having lived near the district police station for three generations and being well-acquainted with most of the local officials - plus the fact that Minh's grandfather had once been a district chief - meant the women could confidently indulge in their beloved 'Tứ sắc' without fear of interference.

Suddenly, the sound of dogs barking came from the front yard. Mrs. Hai leaned over the edge of the divan to peer toward the gate and spotted a young man in plain clothes, whom she immediately recognized as a new secret police officer. Flustered, she quickly turned to her friends and exclaimed,

"Hide the cards, hide the cards!"

Fortunately, the deck hadn't been opened yet. One quick-thinking woman hurriedly took the two boxes of cards into the kitchen and slipped them between the stacked dishes. As it turned out, the officer wasn't there to "bust the game" but to look for Minh. He simply wanted to ask about some details regarding Minh's visit to the temple the previous day with Thành and the two young women.

That night, Minh's parents couldn't sleep, worried that the police's questioning might be tied to some political matter Minh had concealed from the family. Minh, too, was deeply perplexed. Why would the authorities go to such lengths to investigate what seemed like an innocent temple visit by a group of kids?

By the next day, the pieces of the puzzle began to fall into place - or at least, so it appeared from rumors circulating around the neighborhood. Thành and the two young women were suspected of being "undercover operatives" for "the other side." Their temple visit was rumored to have been a reconnaissance mission to find a "meeting location" for their cell's activities.

For more than a month, unbeknownst to Minh, Thành had been living in a rented room tucked away in a house deep within an alley, just a few hundred meters from Minh's home. On the evening after their temple visit, the police launched a raid in an attempt to capture him. However, as the rumors went, "he vanished without a trace." Some speculated that "he was tipped off in advance," which explained why he didn't return to his lodging that night. Others claimed that "he dove into the pond behind the house to escape," using a "water spinach stem" or "a hollow papaya stem" to breathe while submerged.

Minh had no way of knowing the truth behind Thành's disappearance. His heart was restless with worry, fearing that his friend might have been arrested by the police, tortured, and subjected to cruel treatment. Minh was haunted by images conjured from his imagination - of what could happen behind the yellow walls of the former colonial tax office - and the grim reality of political prisoners today, maimed and broken by imprisonment or brutal punishment. He envisioned scenes of prisoners dragging themselves across the ground after being freed from the "tiger cages" - those underground enclosures at the zoo in the heart of Saigon repurposed to hold human captives - or similar iron cages used to detain prisoners on Côn Đảo Island.

This was the dark side of a sudden societal transformation. It was a change that offered opportunities for upward mobility to clients of cunning operators like Ba Đơ, those deemed "pragmatic" enough to adapt to the turning wheels of the era. Yet, like a double-edged sword, those same wheels could crush the unfortunate ones who became obstacles in their path. In these uncertain times, when light and shadow mingled, and truth and falsehood were hard to discern, only conscience and history stood as witnesses - witnesses weary and battered by generations of hatred and chaos.

Judgment by history only holds weight after the chapter has closed. The pages of Vietnam's history, from the division at the Gianh River during the prolonged civil war between the Trịnh and Nguyễn families more than three centuries earlier, have never been truly closed with the ceremonial farewells necessary to heal the wounds in hearts and on bodies, allowing history to move forward. The sacred chants and prayers meant to lay the past to rest remain unspoken, while the future impatiently rushes in to begin.

Chapter 8: Tales of the River

The Gianh River, once a somber marker of division during the Trịnh–Nguyễn Civil War, seemed to have passed its symbolic weight to the Bến Hải River nearly three centuries later. Though their stories may not be directly connected, the Bến Hải, meandering quietly along the human-imposed 17th Parallel, emerged as a haunting new emblem of separation. Fed by streams from the mighty Trường Sơn Mountains and emptying into the Eastern Sea at the Cửa Tùng estuary, this humble river in central Vietnam was suddenly inscribed into history as the line that split a nation in two.

What were once serene childhood playgrounds for Minh and Thành now bore the scars of survival. The ponds and rivers, whether fresh or brackish, had once nurtured plants, fish, and happiness, but now they stood silent, witnesses to stories of loss and endurance. They left behind not only physical divides but also the grieving lines etched into Minh's diary, a tribute to the memory of his late "brother" friend.

Since ancient times, when humans first settled along its banks, the river fostered villages and towns, forming a deep bond with the people. Initially a natural gift, it provided cool water to drink, irrigation for fields, and fertile sediment to enrich the land. Over time, the river became a part of human history, serving as both a witness and a contributor to the creation of folktales - stories filled with pages of tragicomedy, heroism, deep bonds, poetic charm, and, at times, chaos as wild as raging torrents.

Vietnam's rivers are no exception. A 'Bạch Đằng' river of valor, a 'Hát Giang' river of fortitude, have through generations nurtured layers of silt, feeding the spirit of autonomy, the resilience to endure, and the noble sacrifices made to protect a way of life, a principle of existence, and a cultural foundation that has long been the soul of a nation. However, while rivers possess the potential to unite people, they can also serve as sources of division. These barriers may take the form of the romantic notion of lovers separated by the river's flow or as deep-seated as historical rivalries between villages on opposing banks. At times, these divisions escalate into serious conflicts, resulting in loss of life, as history has illustrated.

Nevertheless, amid these complexities, the river remains a unique gift from nature. In regions blessed by its presence, this truth is evident in myriad ways, always. It may materialize in the sight of baskets brimming with fish and shrimp, accompanied by the gentle splashes of freshly caught river treasures, as vendors transport them to market in the late afternoon. Alternatively, it might reveal itself in the excitement of pulling up a trap from the water after rainfall, as the lively sounds of fish leaping to freedom fill the air.

It could also be a catfish wriggling on a fishing hook in the moonlit night, or a voracious snakehead leaping out of the water to snatch the baited hook in broad daylight. Nature's hospitality extends further through feasts prepared by countryside folks for visiting relatives from the big city. They offer a variety of local delicacies, from grilled snakehead fish over a straw fire to freshly boiled snails from the pond, rolled up in rice paper and dipped in deliciously prepared fish sauce.

The river not only nourishes people but also benefits all living things, including plants and animals. At its delta, the river feeds into a stream that flows into a pond, a haven for insects, birds, fish, and various aquatic plants. Along its banks grow reeds, with the sound of crickets chirping in the early morning mist, frogs croaking after the rain, the whistle of a wagtail bird in the summer, or the faint chirping of sparrows every evening as they settle to sleep on the rows of paperbark trees. It's a world of purple water lilies, green water hyacinths, with yellow frogs sitting idly atop. Here, a kingfisher stands with a full belly on the edge of a fishing net pole, gazing at the sky.

Beneath the pond's surface, beside the shade of coconut trees, lies a cluster of finely smooth coontail aquatic plants or a lush green water hyacinth patch, seemingly inviting little fish to play hide and seek along the edge of its cozy white form. On the shore, a few baby dragonflies flutter delicately like strands of colorful thread in the wind, here one moment, gone the next. Or a large, sturdy dragonfly darts around, lively, flying back and forth, paying no mind to the timid golden ladybugs nestled on the water mimosa leaves, flaunting their truly charming transparent 'glass' coats.

In the homeland, the river embodies a spectrum of moods. At times a tranquil haven, lazily winding past groves of coconut trees; at others, a quiet confidant, whispering secrets through the night to the cork tree branches sweeping over the water. Yet, amidst the water hyacinth clusters, adjacent to a resting sampan, behind a menacing French fort, danger lurks.

A French soldier, idly fishing on his boat, may find himself ensnared by the unseen trap lurking beneath the river's surface. With a swift, merciless pull, the trap seizes its unsuspecting prey, dragging him into the abyss. Silence descends upon the river as another life succumbs to its depths, joining the countless others claimed by its murky embrace. Meanwhile, at home, an aging father sits in quiet contemplation, his gaze fixed upon the river, yearning for the return of his absent young son. Despite the calm surface, the river conceals the tragic fate of both perpetrators and victims, swallowing them whole into its unforgiving depths.

Through all the ups and downs of the fluctuating tide, from the days when a girl who rowed the boat ferrying people across the river captivated many young men in the revolution against French colonialism, to the time when she abandoned the helm for the allure of American dollars, the image of the old father waiting for his son at the dinner table in the evening still remains. Feelings may vary, but the heartfelt concerns linger. "If Heaven allows me to meet Hai again, then I'll be at peace even if I have to die," a father confided over the daily cups of rice wine, discussing his eldest son who had long joined the Northern forces. Each generation carries its own sorrows, and the pain of the next generation compounds upon that of the previous one. In this case, the father also had a second son of whom he was proud, a military officer of the Southern forces. Yet, he didn't blame his third and youngest son for buying Paris Match and other English and French magazines every month to supply to his uncle in the National Liberation Front, a proxy branch of the Northern forces, hidden in an unsuspecting villa in the heart of the city. As for the father himself, he remained a loyal civil servant since the French colonial era.

Once upon a time on the 'Cầu Ngang' bridge in a remote countryside, every day, long before sunrise, the sounds of vendors' footsteps rushing to the market mingled with innocent laughter and chatter, dissipating in the early morning mist, as if from some tranquil world. Holding torches, balancing baskets on their shoulders, the farmer's wives brought chickens, ducks, shrimp, fish, vegetables, and sweetened porridge to sell at the market. Suddenly, one day, as they reached the middle of the bridge, the vendors dropped their baskets and fled. On the bridge railing, the head of the Village Chief was found, evidently placed there overnight by someone. A few days later, on the same railing, the head of the culprit was displayed in a similar manner. From then on, every morning, people no longer heard the laughter and chatter of the vendors on the bridge, only seeing the flickering torchlights resembling phosphorous light emitting from graveyards. But with time, everything came to pass. The market had to gather, and it did. What belonged to yesterday now only remained in the memories of the river and in the imagination of a few frightened children, pointing at the dark blood stains on the bridge, teased by adults. The water under the bridge still flowed. Flowing endlessly.

Severed heads displayed on the bridge, blood staining the river, yet the river still flows - continuously flowing. Whether the ferrywoman left affectionate memories in generations of young men during wartime, or whether she departed the river to move on, it still flows endlessly. Temporary changes do not alter the millennia-long process of river formation. The harsh challenges, if just fleeting moments in a nation's history, cannot destroy the state of harmony among people. The river forgives, and people forget.

... Minh wrote it down in his journal as a prayer, a vow.

- The End -

Author

Vinh Quyen Tang, Ph.D., P.Eng..
(Tăng Quyền Vinh)
Ottawa, Canada.

Books published:

1. Bên Kia Bến Đỗ, 2021.
2. Đứa Con An Giang, 2022.
3. Lu nước ngọt, 2023.
4. Nails Tình Thương, 2023.
5. The Boy From An Giang: A Journey Through AI-Assisted Translation, 2023 (Under revision).
6. Tứ Quý (Truyện trích từ Bên Kia Bến Đỗ), 2023.
7. The Precious Quartet (Translated from the Vietnamese title 'Tứ Quý'), 2024.
8. Compassionate Nails: A Journey of Love and Resilience (Translated from the Vietnamese title 'Nails Tình Thương'), 2024.
9. Đôi Dòng Sông Nước, 2024.
10. Tales of the River: Journey from the Mekong Delta, (Translated from the Vietnamese title 'Đôi Dòng Sông Nước'), 2024.
11. Freshwater Jar (Translated from the Vietnamese title 'Lu Nước Ngọt'), 2024.

ISBN 978-1-7381921-9-9